DEATH AT HALLOWTIDE

R.S. Maxwell

ALSO BY SUSAN MAXWELL

Hollowmen
Fluctuation in Disorder

'Hibernia Altera' Sequence
Good Red Herring (Muinbeo Chronicles 1)
A Wild Goose Hunt (Muinbeo Chronicles 2)
And the Wildness (Flux Avellana 1)

SUSAN MAXWELL is an independent author and scholar who writes literary/slipstream and fantasy fiction, and mystery fiction as R.S. Maxwell. She has published five novels and a collection of short stories, and her work has appeared in magazines and anthologies. She has worked as a professional archivist in Ireland, the UK, and the Netherlands, holds a PhD for her research on archives and the margins, and writes non-fiction on themes related to archives and literature. Maxwell is a regular juror for the British Fantasy Awards and reviewer for the *BSFA Review* and *Inis*, the magazine of Children's Books Ireland. Literary influences come mostly from speculative and modernist fiction. When not writing, or painting, or being an archivist, the author can be found in the vegetable patch, listening to music, reading books, watching old detective series, or catching up on sleep.

Praise for *And the Wildness*
"Gorgeous and hilarious and profound." *Siobhán Parkinson*

"A universal adventure story that riffs off Irish mythology … accomplished, intelligent, deeply witty and important … it assumes a thoughtful and imaginative and intelligent reader." *anonymous editorial reader*

Praise for *Good Red Herring*
"Imagine a book like a Pogues concert! Chaotic, powerfully creative … littered with classic and classical Irish references all united in a glorious cacophony of intense delight and beauty." *Nigel Robert Wilson*

Acknowledgements

A huge *thank you* to my persevering band of beta readers. This is the first book for which I have sought the insights of readers prior to publication, and both the book and I have benefitted greatly from their observations.

A brief guide to pronunciation

Áine —— AWN-ya

aos sídhe —— ace shee

bean-feasa —— ban FASS-a

Cecht —— kekht

Corrbofinn —— cor-boh-FIN

Eithne —— ETH-ne

Garda Síochána —— GAR-da shee-okh-AWN-a

Lissascaul —— liss-a-SCAWL

Niamh —— NEE-av

Nuada —— NOO-a-da

Pallasalee —— PALL-ass-a-LEE

púca —— POO-ka

Samhain —— SOW-an ['sow' rhyming with 'cow']

Shanbaltin —— shan-BAWL-tin

sídhe —— shee

Sigune —— SIG-oon

Tír na nÓg —— TEER na NOHG

Tuarashee —— TOOR-a-SHEE

Prologue

Jessica Quill's Narrative. Herne's Acre, Pallasalee, Corrbofinn, Ireland. Thursday 8th September.

I HAD NOT KNOWN what to expect of Herne's Acre. Uncle Tim's solicitor described my inheritance as a 'lodge', so my friends in England had pictured some inglenook-infested charmer in Cotswold stone, transported to a Picturesque-Irish-Village™. Having seen many Irish villages during my first twenty-five years in the land of my birth, I was prepared for a boxy concrete bungalow, with 1970s cladding and a damp kitchen. Herne's Acre was, gloriously, neither.

The road from Dublin's ferry-port to Herne's Acre in the midlands should have been simple. I did not recognise the placenames—the locality was Corrbofinn, the town Lissascaul, the nearest village Pallasalee—but I had a map, a car with sat-nav, and an excellent sense of direction. It would be a cinch.

The first hint that *cinch* was not the word I was looking for came when I turned at a signpost for Shanbaltin Church, and the sat-nav started to sputter. I had it on more for company than anything; the voice had that sort of reassuring cadence like a reader of the shipping news. Barely had the word *Shanbaltin* been uttered when the little device let out a pulsing whoop, and a buzzing jangle of static. Then it went dead. I pulled in as soon as I could, and, unable to get the sat-nav speaking again, I took out the road-atlas.

None of the placenames that I had noted from the solicitor's letter were in the index, nor could I spot them in the pages. I would have to ask for directions. On that ill-kept, fern-whipped boreen, winding precipitously downwards, was a ruined church with a graveyard. As I approached, bouncing from pot-hole to pot-hole, I saw that there was someone among the gravestones.

It was dry weather but the September wind in this exposed place was strong. The woman of whom I demanded help had a scarf wrapped over her face up to her glasses, and a woolly hat almost covered bobbed auburn curls. We exchanged pleasantries about the weather, she waved her plastic container full of shiny dark berries and said it was a cold day to forage sloes, but she wanted to get in ahead of the crowd. With her other hand she took out a mobile phone with a moody black-and-white cover, and reassured me that I had not gone too far off the correct road. She held her phone out so that I could see the map.

It was a bare twenty minutes afterwards that I was driving Gwen the Mini Cooper (yes, my car is named after a *Torchwood* character, thank you for asking) into the yard of Herne's Acre.

The house was a solid two-storey of dark stone. The gable end faced into the yard, which seemed huge to me, and the crimson of the window-frames looked stylish against the blue-grey walls. I parked the car near the back gate, and walked slowly up the muddy gravelled path. To my left was an herbaceous border in full autumn bloom, sheltered by a thick blackthorn hedge. To my right was a thin string of shrubs beside a large wooden shed, and straight ahead of me was a long low building, with windows on each side of the door, all painted crimson.

The large door of the building beside it suggested it was a garage, sheltered by a large tree with—I was somehow astonished as I realised—*actual apples* on it. My sense of smell is unusually acute when it comes to plants, and I knew even from twenty yards away that the apples were ripe, and that they were a heritage variety called Ballinora Pippin. Childishly delighted by the thought of eating an apple straight from a tree that belonged to me, I hurried to select a fruit, and as I bit into it I noticed two other things. One, a large whitewashed dog-kennel, gave me a painful Proustian memory of my lovely Caleb, now six years wherever good boxer dogs go. The other was what lay beyond the wooden fence to my right.

I knew that the property Uncle Tim had left me included a field, but somehow I had not expected it to be so big. I thought 'field' was estate-agent speak, to lure cultivators of tiny suburban handkerchiefs into thinking of a large garden as a field. But it was a few acres, with a thick hedge of blackthorn, hazel, and elm following the curves of the road with a gap for the bridge over the stream, and another thick hedge of elderberry, willow and ash between Herne's Acre and the neighbouring fields. The trees were already on the turn towards winter, some leaves blazing gold and bronze, others green, orange, or deep red. Dark poplar leaves fluttered in the breeze, overturning to flash their bright lining.

The sun glinted on the curve of a polytunnel, and at the back of the field there seemed to be a railing around an overgrown garden. I stood by the gate, chewing my mouthful of apple, and when I had finished, I inhaled as deeply as I could. There were more apple-trees somewhere, there were flowers, I could smell herbs, too: the resinous scent of rosemary, blurry sage, musty hyssop. I was visited by a terrible sense of longing, of regret, even loss, that I could not stay here but would have to return to my life in the suburbs. It felt like coming home just in time to hang up the for-sale sign.

I heard, or thought I heard, the faint crunch of a footstep on the gravel. I looked around. Nothing. Slim-bodied, glitter-winged starlings lined the pitched roof of the house, and corvids perched on the telegraph wires: rooks, magpies, and scald-crows in grey and black. Across the road from Herne's Acre was farmland, and though I could not see the cattle that I could hear lowing, I could see a crowd of trees, which I assumed were the *Heathcote Woods* of the map the solicitor had sent to me.

The thin branches of young birches gave the woods a misty look, and the bright trunks stood out against a smoky, plum-tinted background. I turned back to look at the—*my* —field. Something caught my eye, some slight movement between the willows, their leaves fluttering and whispering. I wondered about a fox, even a hare.

The sound of car-wheels across the gravel roused me from thoughts of impossible things, and I turned as my name was called.

"Jessica Quill?"

Uncle Tim had employed a caretaker for Herne's Acre, one Dermot Thompson, come to show me around and give me my keys. Dermot was about my height with a long-chinned freckled face and strawberry-blond hair.

"Your uncle bought the house and all its contents," he said, leading me to the back door and selecting a key. "I should warn you, it's a lot."

He was not kidding. Dermot had done an exemplary caretaking job: the house was clean, warm, and smelled fresh and sweet. Once inside, a narrow passage led on the right to a bathroom, a small guest bedroom, and a utility area so packed with shelves I could hardly turn in it, and every shelf groaning with *stuff.*

On the other side of the house was an open-plan kitchen, with a solid-fuel stove for heating, an old-fashioned dresser, lots of shelves, and a shining stainless-steel oven with a six-ring hob. The size of the cooker surprised me, as I understood that the last occupant of the house had lived on her own. To the side of the back door, a wooden flight of stairs brought us to the second floor. The door to the en-suite bedroom was next to the window that faced the large and ornate front gate to Herne's Acre, the road, and the high hedge with cattle and Heathcote Woods beyond.

There were three other rooms, each small: one had a settee, music centre, and television, and a big, untidy table at the far end; the second was a library, with just enough room to walk sideways between the shelves; and the third was, to my surprise, a spotlessly neat office. I was sadder and sadder at each room. I could not believe this was mine, and I had to sell it. But everything was in Northern England —my job, my partner, the house, the dog. There was no staying. I turned to smile cheerfully at Dermot, but saw that it was too late, he had seen my real reaction.

"You never know your luck," he said, with sympathy, "there's been rumours that it's been haunted since Hen Rosse died. Maybe you won't be able to sell it."

I laughed aloud. "Thanks for the thought, but ghosts and all, it has to go."

Dermot offered belated condolences on Uncle Tim's

sudden death, and we chatted lightly on reliable topics, like the recent local elections, and the weather, as we walked to his car. I looked around.

"What's at the back of the field?" I asked. "Beyond the stream? Where the railing is?"

Dermot turned to follow my pointing finger, and smiled.

"That," he said, "is your poison garden."

Assistant Principal Officer Thornapple's Narrative.
Commission HQ Offices. Thursday 8th September.

I must be losing my touch—a human nearly saw me. Probably because I slept so poorly last night. Lying awake in the grim pre-dawn, worrying about where these trespassers were getting across, I wondered again about the possibility of Cray being right. One of my trainees, widely known as "Unfortunate Cray," had sidled up to tell me it had been reading about "old tracks," and might that be the problem? I try to encourage even the least promising cases, so I said I would be sure to check, but of course I hadn't. We were busy, busy, busy at the Licence Office all day. So, at three in the morning with no other options, I had decided to investigate Cray's idea the very next afternoon.

At Herne's Acre, I searched meticulously through the boundary hedges, but came away unenlightened. There was something a bit odd in the hedge into Heathcote lands, but I could not make it out. It was when I disturbed the willow leaves that the human seemed to react, peering about, and at one point, looking directly at me. The human, a tall, copper-haired specimen with brown eyes and dimples, was just hanging about when I arrived, and I became suspicious. But then I saw the Caretaker, and of course that told me everything. The ginger must be Tim Fennimore's niece, and the new owner.

Back at the office, I had plenty to occupy my time apart from worrying about humans sneaking to the sídhe side of our border. So, it was not until the long day was over, and I was back in my apartment—a perk of life with the Borderlands Diplomatic Commission—that it occurred to me. A wild idea, maybe, but one that brought me the first spark of hope. Maybe the human had spotted me not on account of any carelessness of mine, but because the human was, shall we say, of the right sort? Might there yet be light at the end of this tunnel?

One

*Jessica Quill's Narrative. Cotter's Lodge, Corrbofinn.
Saturday 22nd October.*

RAIN WAS TEEMING down. Through the uncurtained windows I could see beech trees struggle in the wind. I was visited again by great relief that I had accepted Lorcan Fitzgerald's open-handed invitation to join in the party. Cotter's Lodge was a cheerful place to be, even just for a couple of hours, on so wild a night. As though to reinforce my thoughts, Jamie Conyngham appeared at my side offering to top up my whiskey, and said,

"You got in just ahead of the storm. First one of the season."

He was a handsome young man in a bottle-green suit and a sweet-pea buttonhole I could smell from across the room, so close a friend of the hosts' daughter Delia that he was almost running the party. Delia's birthday was the occasion for the party, and my own stupidity was the reason I was gate-crashing.

"Only just," I said, shaking my head at the decanter. "Good old Storm Gabriel delayed the ferry. I was supposed to be at Herne's Acre hours ago."

Crossing the stream at Chapelraymond Bridge, with Herne's Acre finally coming into sight, had been the moment at which I realised that the keys to the house were still on the table in my gloomy little flat in Durham. After a long trip and a rough ferry-crossing, I could not believe I had landed myself in this complication. I could not even drive Gwen the Cooper into the yard, as the gate was locked.

I had sat for a couple of seconds clenching the steering-wheel, cursing myself, but then pulled myself together. I might be an eejit but I was not a ditherer. I would either have to break into the house, or get a key. A key was simpler. Could I get one? Dermot Thompson—he had a set. I took out my phone.

Dermot was available, but at the party at Cotter's Lodge. My heart sank a little at the prospect of inching around the narrow, winding roads late on a stormy October evening even on so short a trip, but it had to be done. I reassured myself that forty minutes should see me back at the house with a mug of tea. But Lorcan was a come-all-come-any host, Dermot said he was getting a lift later from his sister who would drop me to Herne's Acre, and before I knew it, I was sitting among the Regency cushions of Cotter's Lodge with a plate of food on my knee and a glass in my hand. It was the nicest thing that had happened in months.

Beside me on the settee was Niamh Bracken, whom I had met on my first visit to Herne's Acre. She was a property developer, almost excessively keen to buy my house from me. I had not recognised her; no longer in stretchy cerise office-clothes, she looked very Mae West with a dash of Joan Crawford in grey velvet.

I managed to steer her conversation away from her plans for my inheritance ("take out those trees, except the big ones—knock a few fairy-doors in"), and resigned myself instead to her accounts of trips to Ibiza, and of a row earlier in the evening between Delia's boyfriend Tony Millar and his ex-girlfriend. The noise of chatter made it difficult to hear her, but just as I was running out of platitudes, we were joined by a chap on her other side, got up like a Regency rake and apparently called Ivo, a contemporary of Millar's with whom he had some business connection: renovations or restorations or some "re" word that didn't make it past the whiskey fumes, and he took over the conversational burden.

I got up to bring my plate to the kitchen, but Jamie was already taking it out of my hand. He seemed to be everywhere, though Delia's parents (mostly, I suspected, Karolina) had hired waiting staff, a bartender, and probably someone especially to do the excellent Hallowe'en decorations. There was, however, one thing even the best staff could not do for me, and Jamie directed me to the downstairs lavatory, there being a queue for upstairs.

Cotter's Lodge was a little bigger than the Herne's Acre house, and made bigger again by a glass conservatory that ran the length of its back. Where Herne's Acre was plain and functional, Cotter's Lodge was decorative, more so now with its Hallowe'en trimmings, and Lorcan had told me how he and Karo had re-decorated it on purchase. He had grumbled about how the surveyor's report had revealed all sorts of shoddy practices with the plumbing and electrics —"some cowboy outfit during the Celtic Tiger, no-one was regulating anything"—but clearly enjoyed showing off the original features restored, and the clever ways they had matched the early nineteenth century to their present-day needs.

One item Lorcan had shown me had piqued my interest, so before returning refreshed to the sitting room, I slipped back down the hallway to look again at the glass-fronted cabinet set into a niche in the back wall. It really was a cabinet of curiosities, but all associated with plants and horticulture:

a twisted piece of mandrake for which a dainty-fingered tailor had made some clothes, a wooden bowl with small silver and golden apples, a disc displaying dried leaves of oak and holly.

My attention was slowly brought away from the amber model of a belladonna plant, complete with shining berries, by the sound of a voice. I turned around, and remained perfectly still. It was not, of course, any of my business why someone was pinning Delia Fitzgerald's boyfriend to the wall and angrily hissing into his face, but my instincts have always been towards curiosity rather than politeness. I eavesdropped on the short exchange. The lighting was dim, so of the hisser I could only see her profile, that she was still wearing a dripping raincoat, and her ponytail swinging while she spoke right up into Tony Millar's face.

"…should have known you were always on the make but I swear to God if you say anything, I'll cut your miserable throat for you."

"You got caught out," he hissed back, "and you're up on your high horse when it is all your own bloody fault! Don't you threaten me—"

"They weren't for re-sale—"

"I bought them in good faith," he snapped, and pushed her away. She drew back her arm as though to strike him, but didn't, and they glared at each other like hostile dogs. Then she said he could forget about coming to her for his damn coasters, which seemed a bit of an anti-climax, and strode away. Millar tilted his head about, as though stretching his muscles, and twitchily smoothed his clothes. He leaned against the wall almost defiantly, rubbing his neck while he took out his phone and unlocked it with some brisk tapping.

Millar was a charming distributor of smiles and bonhomie almost equal to Lorcan, who had introduced us on my arrival. He looked like a chestnut, bearded Errol Flynn, twice Delia's age if he was a day, with big brown (but bloodshot) eyes. He wore jeans ugly enough to be designer, and a linen shirt striped in broad multi-coloured stripes. I had an unformed idea that Millar was in business, an entrepreneur, something I never quite understood but which gave the impression of great dynamism and confidence. Delia fawned on him, even after an unpleasant little incident earlier, when Jamie and Karolina had ushered us all into the sitting-room for the birthday cake.

With the lights dimmed and everyone belting out Happy Birthday, they had started unstacking plates, Lorcan telling us how his grandmother had always said an army could march on her boiled-fruit cake. Delia, all wafty faux-mediaeval velvet and drooping wings of hair, was waved back to her seat by her mother, but Ivo got up to help, as did Niamh.

As Jamie passed him, Millar had made a comment about Jamie making a good waiter, laughed, and then slapped Jamie's backside. There was a moment of shocked silence. Karolina said something sharp about Jamie's software company, and bustled everyone back to their chunks of fruit cake, so Millar's next remark was almost, but not quite, covered by the rattling of crockery.

"Didn't tell them it went bust, then, Jamie?"

Jamie ignored him, and shoved a plate of cake at Ivo.

"Ivo has a few bob in the bank, don't you Ivo? With your *special contracts?*" Millar was smiling widely, as bullies do when they want to claim everything is a joke. "Make a good sugar-daddy—"

Jamie had seized a hunk of cake, turned, and shoved it into Millar's mouth. Millar started to choke. Ivo and Niamh each grabbed one of Jamie's wrists, and he let go. Millar coughed out cake, and Jamie thumped him vigorously on the back. Evidently Millar realised he had gone too far, and said nothing.

For those who had seen the encounter, the atmosphere remained tainted until Dermot, nudged to action by Lorcan, demanded Ivo join him in song. Percy French music is not exactly standard birthday fare, but the well-sung silliness worked to bring back the atmosphere.

The party had stayed on track after that, especially as a few guests admitted to having brought musical instruments with them "just in case." All the same, after we had abandoned Percy French and instead reached what felt like the seventeenth verse of *Rocky Road to Dublin*, I felt the need of some quietude, and slipped out. I struck unlucky: I was collared again by Niamh in the kitchen, and somehow a glass of champagne got caught in my hand while she badgered me about selling Herne's Acre.

By the time I had convinced her that I was sticking to my final line—that I had not finally decided what to do, but would let her know if it went on the market—the noise from the sitting-room had begun to dwindle, and the crowd in the kitchen began to grow. People had moved on to drinking shots; I could smell a confusion of botanicals from the drinks. Niamh and I were joined by Ivo Collier, smoothing his damp hair, and his and Niamh's chatter about heritage buildings, special contracts, and grant applications went over my head.

I retreated to the conservatory for a breath of fresh air when Niamh said she must go and have a word with Dermot, and Ivo was collared by a banshee. It was still raining, but not as heavily as when I had arrived. Behind me in the kitchen, people were chatting, some singing, moving about with food and drink. About half the guests were in Hallowe'en costumes, some very convincing: a charred-looking angel, some witches, and 'fairies' in some sort of glimmering make-up. I wondered what was the collective noun for banshees.

It was noisy, and I was tired, but I was glad I was there. Since becoming single abruptly a month ago, I had been living in a charmless short-let flat with my belongings still in boxes. A night of good food, comfortable furniture, and even foolish singing was a tonic.

I began to get cold. Through the back door I saw a witch hurry to a car and climb in, and I wondered when Dermot's sister would come to pick us up. In the kitchen behind me, the voices rose louder, and I saw the bartender bring in a tray of shots, and one of his little helpers—dressed as a goblin —carried a bucket with champagne.

Niamh waved to me across the hallway as she left; Millar was there too, speaking to Ivo who was dragging on his coat, pulling his phone out of his pocket. Delia came up behind them, but Millar spoke to her impatiently. The kitchen seemed to be full of people and movement; Delia trailed sulkily in, hovering by the door while Millar flipped open his phone as he crossed the conservatory. I got up and returned to the noise and warmth of the kitchen.

Then Jamie, unexpectedly behind me, touched my elbow. "Dermot's looking for you," he said, and—being fundamentally more introvert than extrovert—instantly I wanted to be home *now*, curled up with a book, and a cup of tea. I turned to go, and through the open door, saw Millar—inside once more—flashing the charm at a curly-haired banshee in

extraordinary purple ankle-boots. He was within a couple
of feet of Delia. He really had no shame.

In the sitting-room, Dermot waved me over, and we went
to bid farewell to Lorcan. This took quite a while: Lorcan
was tipsy enough to love everyone, and have much to tell
us. While Dermot tried to extricate himself from Lorcan's
volubility, I slipped away. I didn't like leaving Gwen overnight, but I was not fit to drive, and I remembered that my
overnight bag was still on the back seat.

I hurried down the hall, squeezed through the kitchen,
into the conservatory, and out into the wind-whipped yard,
where I fell headlong over Tony Millar, dying in the rain.

Two

MILLAR WAS SLUMPED on his side, his head tucked down. I pulled him by the shoulder, he responded with weak alarm. I called his name, but could feel a creeping dread that there was nothing I could do for him: he was boiling hot, his blood-shot eyes were dilated almost to blackness. He was horribly agitated, but he seemed dazed; his words were meaningless.

I shouted for help, I reached for my phone to call an ambulance, but I must have dropped it when I hit the ground, and it had skittered into the wet blackness. No-one would hear me shouting. I scrambled up to run back in, but Millar was suddenly galvanised, scrabbling like an injured animal. He grabbed my wrist. I knelt down again, not knowing the best thing to do: get help, or stay with one I knew would otherwise die alone.

There was enough light from a window to see him. He peered at me, I held his hand. We maintained this tableau for about thirty seconds. Millar became very still, steadfastly looking me in the eyes. His breath laboured, became a slow hiss. I could smell something on his breath, some dangerous, familiar sweetness.

Millar rasped, his breath a terrible, struggling sound, that dragged into silence. Weirdly, his scent changed: from a peculiarly intense citrus to something faded, burning, like wintergreen. His breath stopped, and he seemed to deflate, as though gravity had released its hold. I let go of his hand. I had started hunting about for my phone when someone said,

"What happened to him?"

"His name was Tony Millar," I said, I don't know why. I was bone-weary and tipsy, my head ringing from the impact of my fall, and shocked at my discovery.

"Are you alright, missus?"

"The smell," I said, sitting back on my heels, "I know it—"

"Let's get inside, missus. You're drenched."

"He was poisoned."

And so it was that I discovered that one of the guests at the party was Detective Sergeant Birhanu. I was too shaken to wonder how he had happened to be by Millar's side with me. He tried to persuade me back into the house, but—shock, I expect—I refused, until the ambulance arrived. I fumbled on the ground for my phone while Birhanu was directing the emergency medical technicians, and I was about to return to the house, but Inspector Butler, or at least a dripping raincape containing her, stopped me.

"Birhanu tells me you diagnosed a poisoning?" she said, and the look she gave me under her hood unnerved me.

"He was still alive when I— found him," I said, my voice shaky. "He was making a noise."

"Speaking?" Butler was very quick with the question.

"No, not words, just burbling. Nonsense. He was very flushed, he was hot to the touch, but there was not a bead of sweat. His eyes were so dilated they looked nearly black, just a sliver of blue."

"And?"

"Hot as a hare," I said, "red as a beet, dry as a bone, blind as a bat, and mad as a hatter."

"He's not the only one burbling," Butler was curt.

"Symptoms of atropine poisoning."

Unfortunate Cray came rushing with the story of the murder. Not a Licensing matter, but anything touching Herne's Acre was my concern.

It had been two years since I was last in the house, when I had had the melancholy duty of attending the Agency's wake for Henrietta Rosse, affectionately known as Hen, our Hosteller for some two and a half centuries. I made a mental note when Cray managed disassembling for once, getting only its tail and one ear caught mid-way through the walls.

"Someone's approaching, chief!"

"Well done, Cray," I said—the little tyke was outdoing itself tonight—and immediately both of us flushed out a camouflage. Though this human looked so exhausted that we could each have split in two and danced a rhumba without causing comment.

JQ put the kettle on, and dug from her pocket the quaint little gadget that they call a phone. She dabbed a couple of times at it, then, to my astonishment, she tossed it onto the table, and cried,

"Ah lads! What is this?"

For one terrible moment I feared she had seen us. She was a stranger to Corrbofinn: the shock would be too much.

"Whose is this?" she wailed. "What else can go wrong— I hate this place! Everything's falling apart and now this!"

Our rules are strict about interactions with unknowing hmans, but I called it an emergency. It took only a touch of magic—the fire crackled more loudly, the rain drummed more heavily, and a small lamp on the piano glowed very gently. A large towel shimmered into existence on the back of the fireside armchair. A bottle, a glass with ice in it, were noiselessly on the kitchen island. I risked a little bit of gentle 'fogging' of JQ's mind, so she did not wonder what was happening. She looked at the fire, and we saw the faintest glimmer of a smile. A hearth-fire on a stormy night. Works every time.

From the suitcase, she fished out some dry garments, and took off her boots. She looked drained, and her eyes in their shadows looked like unpolished amber. Her half-dried hair stuck out at all angles. She sat warming her feet, then rummaged in her case for slippers. With a deep sigh, she got up, poured a whiskey, and stumped upstairs.

JQ was tempted, we could see, to kiss better the wretched day with some entertainment. Some things we from the other side can enjoy second-hand. Whiskey is one of them. Old episodes of *Murder, She Wrote* are another. JQ fell asleep before Cabot Cove's denouement, and I sent Cray home.

I had brought my link with me, so I could keep an eye on activity at the office, but it was all routine, except Personnel's requesting a recommendation for a promotion. I chewed over this. Unfortunate Cray had missed out twice already, but it had improved markedly during its time in Licensing. On the other hand, I had a feeling ours was an environment that suited it. Maybe I was being selfish; I knew who its replacement would be.

JQ woke and staggered off to bed, falling asleep on top of the covers. She did not stir even when I tucked her in, but curled up and slept like the dead.

My sleep that night was not unbroken, exhausted as I was. Probably because of the murder, I had had what my father used to call 'a walker', an intensely vivid dream out of which I would wake up in the place where the dream happened. Like sleepwalking, I always thought, too accustomed to them from childhood to wonder how the locations in the dream and the real world managed to stay in sync.

Fortunately, given the teeming rain, my dream stayed indoors, starting in the utility room downstairs. I woke up at four in the morning standing at the far end of the room with the library. I had not had a walker-dream while I was living with my now ex-partner, and I was surprised at how cheerful the return made me feel. The shelves I had woken up beside stored an impressive collection of detective fiction, my favourite genre, so I had brought *Strong Poison* to bed with me, and snuggled up.

So accustomed was I to the mechanistic routine of being jolted into the day by the alarm, never having had quite enough sleep, that I was shocked when I did not wake up again until half-eight. Having fallen asleep over my book, I slept deeply, and was so befuddled on waking that though I recalled falling asleep on the sofa, and tottering to bed, it was some time before I recalled the dreamwalk, or how I had got back to the cottage. With the recollection of Detective Sergeant Birhanu driving my car, came the recollection of the murder. I wondered if this was what life was like in Corrbofinn.

While I waited for the kettle to boil, I picked up the phone that I had accidentally acquired. I had dropped my phone when I fell over Millar's nearly-corpse. Very likely, he had dropped his, too, when he was overcome by death, and in the dark and the confusion, I had picked up the wrong one. This meant that my phone was hopefully still at Cotter's Lodge, and that I should bring this phone to the guards immediately. Or after breakfast, at least. And maybe after…

I have always been inquisitive, and my friends and co-workers have generally benefitted. In the museums, I puzzled out where 'lost' items wandered to, linked old location lists to new building plans, worked out the identities of un-labelled plants. Even in my hated current job as Facilities Support, I made my way around new equipment, the apparently intractable difficulties of old equipment, recurring problems widely and grumpily accepted as 'just the way it is'. Jejune indeed as they were compared to the conundrums that came the way of a Jane Marple or a Harriet Vane, these problems were highlights in my otherwise soul-sucking day.

It might sound heartless, but Millar's murder piqued this curiosity. I put two slices of bread into the toaster, and took butter out of the fridge. With nothing else to do while I waited, I idly swiped the screen on the phone, and was asked for a four-digit number. I closed my eyes, and thought back to seeing Millar, leaning against the wall of the corr-idor, brushing off the fury of Angry Ponytail. I pictured him, whipping out his phone, tapping in the number. The worst that could happen is that I misremembered it, so quickly, before I dithered, I copied his movements as best I could.

The phone opened.

The first thing that I noticed was that there were very few numbers in it. He was an entrepreneur, however vague that seemed to me; he was sociable to a fault if the row with his ex-girlfriend was any indication. He should surely—

Unless, of course, he had more than one phone, had

different phone for business, for pleasure, for family and friends.

But could this be an entrepreneur's business phone? With five numbers on it? Millar clearly got on the nerves of a lot of people—Ivo told me he thought Lorcan had invited him just to annoy Millar, Angry Ponytail threatened him—but he seemed also to be very charming. Jamie had tried to choke him, but I had seen him turn a bit pink and flustered when Millar made a production of apologising to him later. Delia was besotted. He was a gregarious sort of person. A phone with a handful of numbers suggested secrecy.

I could not resist the temptation. I wrote down the numbers. Then I looked at the calls log, but they all matched. Millar had neither dialled nor taken a call from any number not already in his contacts list. Clearly a phone only for this tight circle of contacts, each number being associated with initials only. BR, MT, NB, MS, TH.

I laid his phone down, but picked it up again for one last question. I had never seen him without his phone in his hand. What was the last number he had used? At 8:58 last night, he had phoned BR.

Three

THE TOAST POPPED, and I laid the phone aside so as to concentrate on my breakfast. I was uncommonly hungry. I would go to Cotter's Lodge to retrieve my phone, and then bring Millar's phone to the guards. I brought down my trusty laptop, and searched the on-line map for directions to Lissascaul via Cotter's Hill.

It was the damnedest thing.

A site popped up immediately, with an azure-blue banner, across which, in white letters, a series of titles passed: *A History of the Surrounds of Corrbofinn, including Lissascaul, Shanbaltin, and Pallasalee*, then *Corrbofinn Weather Channel*, and *Border Commission Updates*. The page that opened was cluttered and difficult to read, the background was dim, and the typeface was diffused, as though it was unravelling. *The history of Corrbofinn*, I read as I squinted, *is hinted at in the first instance by the meaning of the name.*

The writing was too fuzzy to read, and my eye slid away and lit on another paragraph. *Lissascaul is perhaps easier to understand, as* lios *meaning a circular earthen fort is reasonably familiar, and* scáil *is assumed to be the same word that…* but here, the type was so blurred as to be unreadable.

As I looked, the writing and the images receded, and a notification appeared. *Are you resident within Corrbofinn?* I clicked *no*. The notification changed to *No dice, then*. And the website blurred so that it looked like a gauze curtain on a February morning.

I did not know what to make of it. I closed the internet, opened it again, and repeated the search. This time, there was no sign of the site at all. I tried some more searches, expecting that there had to be local government information, something covering things like libraries, the train service to Cotter's Hill and Abbeyduff, the guards. But there was nothing. Complete blank.

It seemed terribly peculiar that a place could exist without leaving some trace on the internet. I knew Corrbofinn only slightly, and I knew that it had a peculiar reputation, but a website only for residents seemed a bit too fussy. I was at a loss for a moment. How would I find information not on the internet? I was old enough to remember there not being an internet, but in my extreme youth, I simply consulted my father, who seemed to know everything in the world, and whose four children treated him as a walking library. Presumably the library in Lissascaul would at least have a map. If I went to collect my phone first, Lorcan would direct me to the garda station. As I shut down the computer, a knock sounded on the door.

It was Lorcan Fitzgerald. He looked the worse for wear, but he would not accept my invitation to come in. Instead, he thrust my phone at me, and said,

"Found it underneath my own car. Good job, saved it from the rain."

I thanked him, and he asked, looking incredibly uncomfortable,

"You alright? After— you know?"

I assured him that I was fine. I asked after his wife and daughter, having a feeling any questions about his own welfare would receive a bluff dismissal.

"Karolina—Karolina, it would take more than a murder

to rattle Karolina," he said. "Delia's another matter. Distraught, she is. In bits. Don't know what to do with her."

"Does she have an idea who might have done it?" I could not resist asking. Lorcan slid a glance at me, looked away, then said,

"Gets crazy notions in her head sometimes. Don't know where— lookit, she's upset, she's just lashing out."

"Who does she blame?"

Lorcan looked miserably at me. Then he seemed to pull himself together. "Leave it to the guards, take no notice of gossip. That's my advice. I've to go, Karo's waiting in the car."

"Can you tell me" I called to him as he started to move away, "is there a garda station in Lissascaul? And which days does it open?"

Lorcan seemed stunned. Then he admitted that there was, that it was open all the time, and told me where to find them, before he positively scurried away. Relieved to have my phone, but bewildered by Lorcan's behaviour, I closed the door.

The garda station was much grander than I had expected. Lorcan had directed me to a modest alley between the library and the social welfare office, an alley opening out into a wide gravelled path that led between two very manicured lawns sheltered by mature beech and chestnut. On the far side of these lawns, there was the familiar blue lantern signi-fying the presence of the guardians of the peace. The building that housed them was a very fine three-storey edifice of red brick. The door was framed by an archway edged with pale sandstone, and its wood and glass looked flimsy for a place associated with crime.

I was very surprised that a rural station in a small town was open all the time, even a Sunday. I approached the long sweep of marble-topped front desk, the soles of my Doc Martens marking in muted squeals my progress across the polished granite.

There were three gardaí behind the desk, looking weirdly stiff and uneasy, in the way that people sometimes look when you have almost caught them doing something they should not. Going up to the nearest one, I said that I had something related to the murder of Tony Millar. I was told to wait. I had barely sat down in the incredibly comfortable armchair before Birhanu was beside me.

"Thank you for dropping in. I hope you are recovered from last night."

"It was a shock," I agreed, "but I'm okay, thanks."

I handed Millar's phone to him. "I dropped my own phone when I fell over him. I mistook Millar's for mine in the dark. I only realised it this morning."

"Where is your phone now?"

I patted my pocket. "Lorcan Fitzgerald brought it back. He'd found it under his car."

Birhanu tapped the phone and the screen lit up.

"My fingerprints will be all over it," I said, "sorry."

He was still staring at the screen, and spoke abstractedly.

"We'll see what it can tell us. Thanks for bringing it in."

"That's okay," I said, and turned to go. This attracted Birhanu's attention, and he looked up to say,

"I'd like to go over your statement in more detail, since you're here. If you'd like to come this way?"

I had given them only a very bare-bones account of my connection to the Fitzgeralds and their party. I followed him up the showy staircase. His office looked a little less glamorous than the reception, but it was still not the cubby-hole I had expected, and he had one of those wooden desks with a green leather inlay. He waved me towards a chair.

"What do you need to know?"

"You arrived at the party at about seven p.m. you said," he was flicking through a notebook. "You didn't see the row that Millar had with his ex-girlfriend."

"No. Dermot told me about it later. He said she had turned up about half five, I think. Broderick, he said her name was."

"When did you first see Millar?"

"Let's see. It took a little while to find Dermot, he introduced me to Lorcan, he invited me to stay. I was a guest by, let's say, twenty-past seven. Then Lorcan brought me to the bar they'd set up, in a sunroom at the side of the house."

The point of a sunroom in this cloudy country escaped me, but to each their own. It was from this room that the drinks flowed at Delia's party, under the stern eye of the bartender. When I had a glass in hand, Dermot had led me to the kitchen while Lorcan returned to his other guests.

"Who did you see?"

The party had started in the afternoon, and so was thinning out by the time of my arrival. Discrete groups began to silt up the comfortable places like the kitchen, a cosy, Aga-heated square of exposed brick with a wooden table accommodating half a dozen people.

"Dermot," I said, picturing my progression into the house, and whom I had met on the way. "Lorcan. Karolina. Delia. Jamie. No—first there was someone who arrived the same time as me."

Birhanu raised his head from the phone-screen, and asked me for the name, his hand poised to write. I thought about it for a second. I had arrived at about the same time as another of the guests, late enough that the only parking spaces had been in a paddock at some muddy distance from the house. She had been just ahead of me, trying to make her way by the light of her phone, her banshee outfit billowing in the high wind. I had a torch, and she had laughed at herself for being unprepared.

"Bridget something," I struggled to remember, "sorry, she spoke softly. Sorley? I saw her later, Millar was flirting with her in the hallway. When we got into the house I saw Niamh Bracken. Then Dermot and the others."

"Anyone else?"

Jamie had guided me to the food, and we met Millar, who invited me to join his group. Jamie said that after a long journey, I would be more comfortable in the armchairs of the sitting-room. Once in the hallway, he warned me that Millar was a sleaze. I told him Millar would be barking up the wrong girl; he said glumly that it was a good call, men were lousers. Once in the sitting-room, I sat between Ivo Collier and Niamh Bracken; I had been a silent presence later when Ivo and Karolina were chatting. I was shaking my head, when I remembered.

"No, but there was someone else." I was childishly excited that I remembered something useful. "Millar had an argument with a woman, earlier in the evening. She was really mad at him, she had him pressed up against the wall."

"Did you hear what the argument was about?" Birhanu looked gratifyingly interested.

"She said… that if he said anything, she'd cut his throat. I didn't hear everything. He said she'd been caught out, that it was her own fault. And she said something about him not being able to get any more coasters from her."

"*Coasters?*" Birhanu looked blankly at me. "Coasters? As

in yokes your ma puts under mugs to stop them making marks on the table?"

I shrugged and held out my hands. "That's what is sounded like. There were a few people there involved with, like, renovations and house design and stuff. Maybe something to do with—antiques? Something like that?"

Birhanu did not reject the suggestion, but he looked very doubtful. Still, I did feel I had given him a clear suspect.

"Did you witness an altercation between Millar and Niamh Bracken?"

"Niamh? No," I cast my mind back, "I don't think I saw them together at all."

"This would have been outside, just after she left?"

I shook my head. "No, but if it was, it can only have been about half an hour or so before I found him—she left around nine."

"Okay," he nodded. After a long-ish silence, he said,

"Tell me again about Bridget—Sorley, was it? How do you know her?"

"I don't. I met her by chance when we arrived at the same time. We just made small talk for the minute or so it took to get to the house She said she was meeting a friend."

"Might that have been Millar?"

"I don't think so. I only saw her speak to him once. After the whole business with the cake, before I went in to say goodbye to Lorcan. I saw Millar through the doorway, being very flirty with her."

"Was she flirting back?"

"Hard to tell. Maybe she was just being polite." She had been leaning against the wall, swinging an empty shot glass between her fingers, smiling. "She looked kind of bored, really."

Birhanu nodded thoughtfully, and went on nodding as though he had forgotten to stop.

"We don't have her on the guest list," he said abruptly. "No-one called Bridget anything."

"She must have been invited," I objected. "You don't deck yourself out for Hallowe'en and start crashing parties in the middle of nowhere. One of the Fitzgeralds will know her."

We looked at each other. I was not sure what he expected me to say.

Four

Birhanu continued. "Would you recognise Angry Ponytail again?"

"I doubt it. I only saw her silhouette."

"Anyone see you talking to Bridget Sorley?"

"Well—I don't know, I don't think so," I was a bit startled at the question. He seemed to be jumping about a bit. "No, hang on, Niamh Bracken did."

The front door had been on the snib and when I pushed it open, there was Niamh. She had greeted me like a long-lost pet, but eyed Bridget down and up so that Bridget touched her shiny hair and straightened her costume, her movement wafting her faintly cherry scent towards me.

"When you were upstairs, did you happen to look out of any window overlooking the back of the house?"

"I wasn't upstairs."

"We had a witness who saw someone outside, near the cottage behind the house, where Delia lives."

"Can't help you. I didn't see Angry Ponytail in the house again, maybe it was she. I'm surprised anyone saw anything, the night was dark as the pit, and raining."

"The windows were uncurtained," Birhanu pointed out, "light coming into the yard from all angles."

"Is that how you saw Millar?" I asked suddenly. "You turned up just when I found him. Did you see him?"

"I heard you shouting for help."

"How could you have heard me? The doors and windows all shut, and the wind hooting?"

"I have very good hearing," he sounded very shifty.

"You'll be part bat, then," I retorted, and wondered if you could be arrested for sarcasm to a garda sergeant.

"You didn't see anyone in the vicinity before you found Tony Millar, is that right?" Birhanu sounded dignified. When I said *no*, he shuffled his papers, and said,

"You say that you were in the conservatory after the music started, and you were alone there. You didn't go outside at any point?"

"Not until I was leaving, no."

"You did not go up to the cottage that he shared with Delia?"

For a moment, I was too startled to answer.

"I didn't know where— no, of course not, why would I?"

"Did you have any quarrel with Millar?"

"No, I never met him before."

Birhanu did not say anything for a moment or two. Then he spoke briskly.

"You are staying at Herne's Acre, aren't you? We will need to speak to you again."

I was somewhat unsettled by the don't-leave-town vibe of Birhanu's final words, and felt in need of a restorative coffee, though I hardly expected any cafés would be open on a Sunday. Lissascaul was a small town with a long history. Like many rural towns, it had taken a battering during the recent recession, but was beginning to show some sparks of life again, with traffic disrupted by building works, signs announcing businesses re-opening. In the middle of the town, there was a small, pretty square on one side, and Briody's Café on the other. It was open.

I parked Gwen beside a memorial with flowerbeds, and trotted over.

There was even a short queue. I glanced around the café while I waited, and in between admiring the art deco style, I saw that one of the tables was occupied by Niamh Bracken. I felt the urge to talk to someone about the murder, to put Birhanu's disconcerting words into perspective. I had never been shy, but I am cautious of new people. I made a deal with myself—if Niamh was still there when I had my coffee, I would join her. She was, so I did.

"Good morning to you," she said. "What a night, eh? I can't believe I was gone before it happened."

"You left around nine, didn't you?" I settled in. "It wasn't long after that."

"I don't recall the time I left."

"I heard you had a bit of a run-in with Millar."

Niamh, for a fleeting moment, looked almost scared.

"Oh, that," she was cheerful. "You know what he was like —any opportunity for a quick flirt. I didn't notice the time."

It had not sounded like a quick flirt, the way Birhanu spoke about it. And a conversation lasting several minutes cannot have been comfortable for Niamh in high heels on gravel. But maybe she thought it was worth it to tear a strip off him for his manners.

"I hear *you* found the body," she said, and through a mouthful of scone, I told her what had happened.

"That must be why—"

She stopped so abruptly I thought she was choking.

"Why what?"

The pause stretched on. Then Niamh said,

"Look—Delia was just crazy about Millar. I mean, she wasn't reasonable. You saw what he did, grabbing her arm like that. But she was just… enamoured. He could charm anyone. So, I suppose…"

"What?" Would she never spit it out?

"If you were the one who found Millar dead, then that might be why Delia is saying you killed him."

If she had said Delia accused me of shooting boxer dogs, I could not have been more astonished, or more outraged. Before I had a chance to speak, Niamh hurried with reassurances: Delia was clearly overwrought, the guards would never believe her, I had no motive.

She was right, of course. Delia seemed besotted with Millar. She tolerated everything, even the nasty little display of aggression that Niamh referred to, when Delia had reacted with annoyance for once to Millar's flirting with someone, and had stalked off. Millar reached out and grabbed her arm, twisting it up her back and nearly pulling her off her feet, pushing her behind him.

Millar had flicked a glance around the shocked guests, smiled smugly, and put his hand on Delia's face. Instantly, she was all simpers and giggles. The expression on Jamie's furious face said that he had seen this before. Lorcan was standing irresolute in the doorway, with Karolina behind him. But would Delia's lovestruck state be sufficient in itself for the guards to dismiss her accusation against me?

"I didn't even know Millar," I said, "I had no reason to kill him."

Niamh held up her hands.

"Don't shoot the messenger. Like I said, you've no motive."

"Plenty of people there did have motive," I was still indignant. "Delia, if she came to her senses. Jamie—Millar humiliated him."

"The ex-girlfriend, what was her name? Gemma something?"

"Broderick, I think. Delia's parents, maybe."

Niamh scrunched up her face. "They were on Team Millar, oddly. How about Ivo Collier? He and Millar didn't get on, there might be something there."

"A business connection, wasn't it?"

"Yes—Collier does these high-end renovations, Millar was a supplier. Collier caught him out with some shady practice or another, called him out publicly over it."

"What practice?"

Niamh shook her head. It sounded to me more like a motive for Millar to kill Collier, but then I wondered. Maybe Collier and the Ponytail were connected somehow? I described Angry Ponytail, but Niamh had not seen her.

"Poison's a difficult way to kill someone at a party," I reflected, forgetting that this means was not either common knowledge or even a certainty.

"Was it poison?" Niamh almost pounced.

"I think so."

"No chance it was an accident?" she said, and I shook my head

"I don't think so," I told her, "not if I'm right that it was atropine. It isn't the kind of thing you just have in your pocket."

"You know about poisons?" she sounded incredulous.

"I do," I said.

I had loved my time as an undergraduate, but I had arrived on the job market in Ireland armed with an entirely generic humanities degree, just in time for an economic boom to hike the rents, and for employers to discover the benefits of hiring temporary contractors instead of employees.

I took the well-worn trail to London, taking a job as assistant in a *materia medica* museum near Cheapside. I loved it, but after a while, knew it too well to be stimulated by it. Then Bethune Abbey in Surrey were looking for an assistant in their museum. Soon, Pup Caleb and myself relocated to Dorking, and I was taking coffee-breaks with people who had worked in the Bethune Physic Garden for twenty years. I knew a *lot* about plants, medicinal and poisonous.

"Do you know someone called Bridget Sorley?" I asked.

Niamh shook her head again.

"She and I arrived at the same time. Curly hair, glasses, dressed like a sort of Celtic Twilight banshee. Velvet boots."

"Oh, the Cavellettis! Gorgeous."

She waved her foot at me, in a glossy yellow shoe with a vertiginous heel.

"I remember the boots, don't remember who was in them."

For some reason, Niamh's failure to recall Bridget made me uneasy. Then her phone rang, and she excused herself to answer it. The conversation was very brief, and very terse on Niamh's side.

"Sorry," she said to me as she got ready to leave. "Nice chatting—you have my number when you're thinking of selling."

I finished my scone thoughtfully.

The more I thought about it, the more difficult it seemed to work out how you could poison someone at a party. People are changing places, changing drinks-glasses, plates, all the time. You had to come prepared, too. It was not difficult to extract atropine from the belladonna plant, but how to get someone to ingest it? How could any of them —Angry Ponytail, Jamie, Gemma Broderick, Ivo, Niamh, even—possibly have done it? My own money was on Angry

Ponytail, who openly threatened him. She was aggressively close to him too—injection?

I brooded over my coffee. Finally, I pulled myself together. If Delia Fitzgerald was trying to collar me, I would have to beard the lion in her den.

Thornapple's Narrative. The Wing and Claw Tavern, Sunday 23rd October.

It being a day off, I took a long lunch with Sigune in the Wing and Claw, a favourite haunt of ours. Sigune, one of our more disreputable diplomats, was in disgrace again (another spat with the Master of the Wild Hunt). I told her everything I knew about the murder, to cheer her up, but also to stay within her invaluable gossip-economy.

The crime disturbed me less than you might think. Corrbofinn is not a violent place. But it is not tranquil, either. There are crossing-points between the human world and the sídhe, and all sorts of 'otherworlds'. Some borders are not very… official. Some people, on both the sídhe and the mortal side, resent the Commission's attempt to regularise travel between the two. We have agents constantly on the trail of the traders in untracked antiques, boosters and drugs, suppliers of everything from silver apples to xenomorph pets for the "sídhe exotica" market.

I had spent the whole morning with our Watchers, checking reports, requests for passes and licences, trying to track down our local trespassers. Corrbofinn is one of the biggest such crossing points on this island, and we are eye-wateringly official. We are the Borderlands Diplomatic Commission, up to our ears in diplomats and bureaucracy. But…

We are approaching the Season of Shades, and the fur on my neck is already bristling. We never get a moment's peace from Hallowtide to Twelfth Night. There are those who say I am pessimistic, but I say *experienced. Practical.* Between Sundown on Hallowe'en and Sunup on Little Christmas, anything can happen, and it usually does. We seem to have started early this year.

Five

Jessica Quill's Narrative. Cotter's Lodge, Sunday 23rd October.

KAROLINA ANSWERED the door of Cotter's Lodge. She looked exhausted, but elegant, in various shades of pale grey. She seemed surprisingly unsurprised to see me.

"I suppose you heard," she said, wearily. "Would you like tea? Or I have just made fresh coffee? Please do say yes," she urged, when I hesitated. "Delia's hysterical, and Lorcan is fixing something that is not broken. It would be a relief to speak to someone not in an extreme state."

I followed her down the hall. There was a garda standing in the doorway of the sunroom, and I glimpsed figures at work inside. The drawing-room was similarly protected, and part of the kitchen was still cordoned off while people in white hooded overalls were creeping about the place, measuring, making notes, peering through magnifying glasses.

The framework of investigation spilled out from the kitchen, across the stretch of dew-sodden grass, and through the slow-moving figures I could see the crooked little cottage that I assumed was Delia's. From somewhere in the house came the sounds of a hammer. Karolina hurried me out to the conservatory, and then joined me, bringing the coffee.

"How is Delia? Apart from thinking I killed Millar."

"In tears," Karolina sighed, "all the time. There's nothing I can say. If they had broken up, we could just ride out the storm. Everyone gets their heart broken. We'd know what to do."

She made a face, and inhaled the scent of the coffee. I don't know anything about coffee, but it did smell very delicious.

"But murder… I don't know how to help her. At least her brother and sister are on their way."

"Karolina, why is she accusing me?"

Karolina came back with the coffee-cups, and sat down with a deep sigh.

"Delia is convinced that you were having some row with Tony over Herne's Acre. There was some agreement that went sour, someone owed money."

"I didn't—"

"I know. Really, only Delia. Personally, I wondered if it was an argument with Ivo Collier that she overheard."

"Ivo Collier? Why?"

Karolina sighed again.

"Lorcan is too mischievous sometimes," she said affectionately, "he would not have invited Ivo at all if Ivo had not publicly scarified Millar for raising his prices."

"I suppose things just become expensive," I said doubtfully, but Karolina shook her head decisively.

"Ivo does renovations, very high-end, specialist projects," she said. "Half-way through Ivo's highest-profile job, when he couldn't get another supplier for—well, his more specialist requirements, Millar nearly doubles the price."

Motive? I wondered. Ivo seemed very urbane for a murderer.

"Maybe that was who Delia heard," I said blandly, and Karolina smiled at me, and said,

"I hope you were not too upset. Finding a dead body must have been a bit… startling."

"Not an everyday event," I agreed. "Though strictly speaking, he wasn't dead when I found him, he died a few minutes later."

"No last words, no naming his killer, or saying 'the treasure is buried…'? Oh, I shouldn't make light of it, but I am at a loss, an unfamiliar place for me."

"Is Lorcan… I mean, can Lorcan…?"

"I hear IKEA do chocolate teapots now," Karolina said, salty as hell, "but hey, I've got mine."

I wasn't sure whether to laugh or not, and she added,

"I shouldn't be harsh. But it is intensely emotional around here, and that is not Lorcan's forte. Not really mine, either, but one of us has to deal."

"Delia seemed very… taken with Millar."

"Delia has been like a half-witted child," Karolina said, firmly. "She's twenty-five, not sixteen. Once Millar was on the scene, she turned into mimosa, all clingy and limp."

She drained her coffee. "I have never liked mimosas. We all thought him incredibly charming, but funny enough, with him gone, my recollections are not charming at all."

"Can I ask—do you recall a guest of yours, called Bridget? Surname might be Sorley?"

Karolina laughed.

"Lorcan asked me to do the guest-list," she shook her head, "insisted he was going to be *very strict* about sticking to it. I can assure you that you were far from the only un-planned guest. All I can say is, I didn't invite anyone called Bridget anything."

"He's a very generous host," I said, and Karolina smiled very sweetly and said that Lorcan in sociable mood would invite the devil himself.

"There is one thing I want to ask you, though," she added,

"it has been bothering Delia very badly." She blew out her lips, in a determined manner. "Was Millar suffering when he died?"

"Oh, look," I protested, "I'm not a doctor, I can't …"

"Please, just give me something I can tell her."

"I don't know. All I can say is… Look, if it was atropine that killed him, then it is not, as far as I know, painful in the way that, say, strychnine is, or cyanide. Your heart rate goes right up. You can't sweat, so you are very hot. He was probably hallucinating, he was rambling. He didn't show signs of pain. His eyes were dilated but that doesn't hurt…"

I trailed off, puzzled. Karolina nodded. She seemed relieved. "I can tell her that, then."

"They were *blue*," I recalled aloud, and turned to Karolina. "Millar had brown eyes, didn't he?"

"Yes. Delia thought they made him look like the poet Shelley."

"When I turned him over, Millar's eyes were really dilated, but what I could see of the iris was blue, bright blue."

Karolina turned right around in her chair, and said with extraordinary emphasis,

"Oh, *was* it?"

She turned back, staring out at the wet garden with an expression that suggested someone might get a horse's head on their pillow before the week was old. She rattled her cup into her saucer.

"Come and say hello to Lorcan. I need to get some bits together."

I hurried after her, back into the house, and down the passageway where I had seen Millar and Angry Ponytail. The hammering became louder, and Karolina knocked on a door next to the cabinet of vegetable curiosities that I had admired on the night.

"Lorcan told me the house took a good bit of work," I said, over Lorcan shouting a reply.

"I was heartbroken when we got the surveyor's report," Karolina opened the door. "I loved this house the moment I set eyes on it. The owner baulked but Lorcan made a fair offer, considering how much it took to fix it."

What Lorcan had been hammering, up a ladder in a utility room, was anyone's guess. I hovered outside while he descended from the ladder, immediately complaining about the guards asking him impossible questions about whether he had seen anyone lurking around the cottage shortly before Millar died, but Karolina cut right across his rant.

"Millar was using boosters, Lorcan."

Lorcan stopped dead, staring at her. He was taller than either of us, with a high, florid colour in his cheeks. His shirt was bright enough to warn off predators.

"What's a booster?" I asked, but Lorcan was already giving vent to his revised opinion of Millar. His vocabulary was extensive, uninhibited by any anxiety about speaking ill of the dead man whom he intended digging back up, once buried, to give him a good kicking.

"I need to make herbal tea for Delia," Karolina said, unlocking a press and taking down some jars, and a mug, "why don't you explain to Jessica about boosters."

Lorcan looked at me, then back at Karolina, and said awkwardly,

"But she's not from here."

"Either she'll stay and need to know," Karolina said mysteriously, "or leave and forget."

"Boosters are a sort of drug," Lorcan said shiftily. "Not exactly illegal, but... a menace to others when used by the likes of Tony Millar."

"What do they do?" I asked. If Millar was in the habit of drugging his girlfriends, I was less surprised that someone had slipped him some atropine.

"When you take them, they… affect the judgement of people you interact with," Lorcan said, after a struggle to find the words, and Karolina piped up,

"It would explain why Delia was *quite* so drooping in his presence. She is often spineless if she thinks it will make people like her, but this was ridiculous."

"Karolina, you're being too hard on the girl."

"Nonsense, Lorcan," Karolina said firmly, putting down the mug. "She needs to stop trying to please people. It's an invitation to nasty types like Millar."

"I thought you two were on Team Millar," I said, and they both turned to me. Lorcan grumbled that the little bleep wouldn't have got his bleeping foot in the door without boosters. He turned on Karolina's instruction to put some water on to boil, while Karolina was taking herbs from the jars and measuring them into a muslin bag.

Not wanting to interrupt, I took another look at the cabinet. In the brighter light of the day, I could see more of the contents. There was a dark-green perfume bottle in a very ornate silver holder, a small heavy-bottomed drinking-glass, like a grubby medicine dispenser with a golden rim, and a triptych of pressed flowers: mallow, sweet violets, and poppy.

I jumped a little when Karolina was suddenly beside me. She was holding the mug, full of steaming liquid, and frowning into it.

"Damn it, I can't remember if I put in the chamomile."

I looked, too, and inhaled deeply.

"You did," I said. "You have chamomile, St John's Wort, lemon balm and— what's the last one? Milk thistle?"

Karolina stared at me like I had sprouted a third eye.

"That's some nose you have," she said, and turned to go up the hallway. "I don't mean to be rude, but I have to go and see Delia."

I went back into the workroom, and told Lorcan I would get out of their hair. I did not mention that I had just had an idea.

"I wonder, though," I asked as he joined me to escort me to the door, "did you see one of your guests get into a row with Millar? Not Jamie, a woman."

"His ex? Gemma?"

"No—a woman with a ponytail. Blonde. I don't think she stayed long."

Lorcan was shaking his head. "I've a terrible memory, though. I'll ask Karolina."

I assured him at the front door that I did not take offence at his daughter accusing me of murder, but just before I left, I said,

"Just one last thing."

"Ha! *Columbo*!" he said, unexpectedly, and then added, "My mother used to love *Columbo*."

"Do you know where I'd find Gemma Broderick?"

"I don't think she had anything to do with it. She was gone the minute she saw him snogging Delia. Well, after she'd insulted him. Colourful language, has Gemma."

"I just thought she might have some idea who else had it in for him."

"Don't worry about it, the guards aren't going to take Delia seriously. Sure, what motive had you?"

I did not like to tell him about the suspicious look in Birhanu's eye when I left. "Call it curiosity. A Miss Marple complex."

He thought for a minute or two, and finally said, "I'm told she takes her fiddle to the trad session they do have down in Whalen's in the village."

Six

I RETURNED TO Herne's Acre for lunch. Unpacking my shopping, I pondered my next move. Going to the pub to see if I could track down Gemma seemed like a start, assuming there would be a session in Whalen's before I had to return to England. I was cherishing a hope that Gemma might turn out to be Angry Ponytail. I planned to call Birhanu, to explain that what I heard as 'coasters' might in fact have been 'boosters', but I liked the idea of being able to say that I had a name where before I had only a hairstyle.

I measured out some rice and put it on to cook. I had bought some smoked fish, and this I put on to simmer gently. I had seen shoes that were bigger than the kitchen in my short-let flat in Durham, and, with only a microwave to make do with, I had been eating ready-meals so often that I relished even this temporary access to a decent kitchen.

Or maybe I could not really blame the small kitchen. When my lovely job in Surrey had fallen victim to the economic crash, right after my beloved Caleb died, I had met Louise and moved north to Kirkaller very quickly. I had been glad to get even the appalling job I did have, but it meant a long commute and a lot of stress and boredom. Life had seemed just too *much*, and I had picked up Louise's habits of eating out, eating fast, eating convenient. Five years on, I wondered if my newly single state should signal a return to my old habits.

Just as the fish began to simmer, someone knocked on the door.

When you work in a place where you interact with members of the public, you very quickly learn how not to be surprised at anything you see. In the museums, we had a lot of poisons, pre-industrial plant medicine, and historical information, including information about murders. We had all sorts of visitors: academics, Goths, hassled researchers from television detective series wanting to know how much digitalis you needed to eat before it was fatal, historical re-enactors, sometimes in costume, novice witches, folklorists, at least one Satanist.

Neither of my bosses had tolerated the slightest smirk at anyone's choices, and since I have no tickets to anyone else's life, I've been happy to jog on. All this stood me in excellent stead when I opened the door to what appeared to be Dick Turpin, complete with thigh-boots, but with acid-green hair, a carefully painted glittery mole on the cheekbone, and a definitely punkish, Tenpole Tudor sort of air.

"Hi," said Tenpole Turpin, "are you Jessica Quill? Great— I'm Molly Thompson. Dermot's sister."

I offered her tea, which she refused, but she did sit down, pulling off her gloves.

"I hope you can help me," Molly said. "I need to buy some fresh herbs, and I know October is a terrible time of year for it, but I was wondering…"

"Um—sure. I mean, as you say, the dormant season's not great, so it'll depend on what's growing here and how much you need."

"I won't need much," she assured me, pulling a list out of her pocket, "and just small amounts."

I looked at her list. She added, as if it needed explanation,

"It's just that Hen's herbs were really first-class quality. She had a business based on them, I suppose you know?"

"No, I didn't."

"She sold them, made oils and tinctures and stuff. She had wonderful stock."

"Why don't you leave it with me? I'll have a look, and let you know."

"I was kind of hoping…"

I looked at her, and her curly smile faded. "If I give you my phone number," she said, writing quickly in a small notebook and tearing off the page, "could you call me about it?"

"I will." I picked up my phone, and keyed in the numbers she gave me. "I will let you know as soon as I know how I can help."

Molly seemed faintly dissatisfied, presumably because I had not dropped everything to answer her request, but she thanked me, pulled back on her gloves, and got up to leave.

"Terrible business about this Millar man," I said, just making conversation on the way to the door, and she immediately tensed. Very slightly, I might not have noticed except that she was in profile as she passed through the door I was holding open, and I saw the twitch of a frown, the tightening of her lips.

"Terrible. I didn't know him personally—mostly heard he was pretty awful, but you know… murder."

"Did you know Ivo Collier?" I said on impulse. "I heard he had a row with Millar—"

"I heard he had a go at him, alright," she shrugged, "but that was months ago. He's hardly a suspect. Ivo? He wouldn't risk any scandal getting back to—"

There she stopped. She stared at me for a few seconds, then abruptly thanked me, and left. As soon as I finished my lunch, I went upstairs to the office, looking for a large piece of paper.

Hen Rosse may have had a borderline-chaotic approach to other areas of the house, but her office was impeccable. There was a drawing-board between the two windows, with a beautiful, hand-drawn plan of an herb garden. I wondered if it was the poison garden, but the legend at the bottom of the page told me that these herbs, including the ones Molly Thompson had asked for, were to be found in Carnsore Glass-house. The sight of it brought back a rush of affectionate memory of the drawings and maps we had for the Bethune Physic Garden, and also that stab of longing, of homesick-ness, of wanting to stay in Herne's Acre.

I resolutely put the paper and the associated emotions aside, though when I found a sheaf of hand-drawn plans I could not help admiring their elegance, and their remarkable level of detail. Hen's decision to name her glasshouses and polytunnels after shipping zones—Carnsore, Rockall, Fair Isle—endeared her to me. Under the plan I found exactly what I was looking for: a large sheet of graph paper.

The office was a bright, comfortable room. The window at the back looked out over the hedge that separated Herne's Acre from the Heathcote land. I could just see the chimneys of Heathcote among the trees of its eponymous woods. I wondered how extensive their farm was, and what the people living there—the Hearne family—were like as neighbours. Through the window that faced the front of the house, I could see a few cattle in the field and, with a slight squint, part of the blackthorn hedge that marked the edge of my property.

Whereas the days that follow a big storm are often bright, today, despite Gabriel's passage overhead, was murky and dull. Even now, the early afternoon light had an ashy quality. All the trees looked like ink smeared on a sepia paper, with sooty smudges of birds. In a way, it was a dreary sort of day, but none the worse for that when you have a quiet, neat room to sit in, and a murder to solve.

I started with a sketch-plan of Cotter's Lodge. Then I listed down the side of the page all the people I knew had attended the party, marking with a red asterisk those whom I thought had motive for murder.

I supposed Lorcan and Karolina might have resented Millar's treatment of their daughter but Niamh had told me they had been Team Millar. Karolina had said *charming*. Anyway, if Lorcan had become murderous, I could not see him fossicking about extracting atropine—actually, there was a thought. I had been in their workroom so briefly that even my sense of smell could not identify everything in Karolina's herb-cabinet. But if she used plants medicinally, probably she kept medicines that could also be poisons. Her cabinet had been locked, after all. But still. If Millar had been found bludgeoned—or strangled with his own left leg, as per Lorcan's vigorous plan when he heard about the boosters—Lorcan might have sprung to mind.

The look on Karolina's face when she realised that Millar had been using these *boosters* to get a hold over Delia gave me pause for thought. I would not have put it past her. On the other hand, she did not know about the boosters until after Millar's death. My red pen hovered, but I did not mark Karolina's name.

Who else? Jamie. He resented Millar's treatment of Delia, and had also actually attacked him in retaliation for Millar's humiliating 'teasing'. Lashing out was not pre-meditated murder, though. Poison was pre-meditated. Jamie had plenty of opportunities given he was a friend of Delia's, why would he commit murder in public? Maybe the party had been the last straw. Maybe he had thought about it, and then the party saw the red mist descend. He got the poison—from where? He administered it—how?

Assume Karolina did have atropine. Jamie would know about it. Millar goes too far. How long between the cake incident and Millar's death? Atropine could kill in ten minutes, it could take half an hour. Jamie was out and about a lot during the party. Someone was seen in the vicinity of the cottage—when was that?

On a shelf under the drawing-board I found a pad of paper. I took a sheet, and began to write down the questions.

Niamh Bracken—did she have a motive? Birhanu told me of a row between Niamh and Millar, Niamh had lied about Millar flirting with her, to cover up. Could she have had an opportunity? She had left about half an hour before Millar died, but how long had she been talking with him outside? He might have already been showing signs of symptoms before she finally left. But then he had also been pretty drunk. Every time I saw Millar he seemed to have a different kind of glass in his hand, and Dermot had made a quip about the metal from which Millar's liver must have been made that could handle everything from absinthe to Zombies.

Who else had we?

Angry Ponytail. She had threatened to cut his throat, if he said something. About what? What was her own fault? She was involved with these 'booster' drugs, whatever they were, and she had threatened to withhold his supply. Or—here was a thought. Could the atropine (assuming I was right about that; I had to keep reminding myself it was not definite except in my own head) be administered via these boosters? I had never taken drugs, aside from alcohol and caffeine, so my knowledge of procurement or use was based on films like *Trainspotting* or *Boogie Nights*, and the cinematic was little use in answering the practical. On my question paper I wrote *How to identify Angry Ponytail?*

Inspiration of a sort struck. It was not an answer, but it might be a thread. In the bedroom, I had left a little pile of random odds and ends—keys, receipts, shopping list—and among these I found the scrap of paper on which I had written the phone numbers and initials I had found on Millar's phone. Might any of these be Angry Ponytail? If they were then it suggested that the connection between them was a business one. Millar was an entrepreneur, infuriatingly vague as a job description.

I re-read the initials. I thought of phoning one of the numbers, but then dismissed the idea. Who knew who I would end up talking to, and besides, I had a feeling that the guards would not be pleased. Butler was scary enough even when she was neutral towards me, I did not want to see her angry.

I looked back at my plan of the house, and back at my list. Karolina had told me that Delia's accusation of me had something to do with business—did that inch Collier into the picture? Might a working hypothesis be that Angry Ponytail was in the same business? I felt a spark of pleasure at this advance in my problem, but it was quickly doused. I could hardly go about claiming to want renovations just to see if an angry woman with a ponytail got in touch.

Seven

*Thornapple's Narrative. The Wing and Claw Tavern,
Sunday 23rd October.*

"Well, well. This is a turn-up for the books, as they say."

Sigune was on the hunt for more gossip. She is a decent skin, and a friendly ally, but has been in the service so long that her bad habits are irreparable, and her abilities with diplomatic double-speak are a bit moth-eaten. She often gets her knuckles rapped, and gets moved to administrative duties till she remembers her manners. She was currently on one such time-out, seeing out her punishment in my office, signing off access passes, clearances, requests for air-traffic. She likes Licensing. Says a better class of biscuit arrives with the morning tea.

"Our new Hosteller is none other than Timothy Fennimore's niece? Have some devilled eggs."

"We don't know that she is the Hosteller, yet," I tried to warn her, but she was off, reminiscing about Fennimore's skills that had been so valuable to us on his particularly tricky patch in the Cheviot Hills.

"There will be trouble on *our* patch if we don't have a Hosteller at Herne's Acre."

"Sigune—look, there is always trouble, on everyone's patch. Outside the Commission, there are those who want to see us fail, there are those who want to take advantage of our network between worlds. Inside, we heave with examples of ambition that is greater than skill, with colleagues whose greatest talent is grabbing the spotlight with other people's work. You know this. Fennimore knew it, too."

There wasn't much she could say to that. I was right, and besides, her mouth was full of devilled egg.

"All the same," Sigune said, egg dispatched, "Fennimore has left us in a unique position. A Hostel has never been left to anyone who did not already know what that meant."

She took some more egg, and before she had finished chewing it, added,

"A Hostel has never been *left* to anyone at all. Not in a legal sense, where they could decide to sell it. I expect Fennimore intended to explain himself, to us and to his niece. Death is so irresistible a caller."

Fennimore had been a very able and subtle diplomat, and a person of great integrity and excellent judgement. That was why he tended to be posted to the more unstable and fractious of our Borderlands, across Ireland and Britain, and from Scandinavia to Iberia. That was why he landed in East Lintzfield, beginning to become notorious. In an Agency full of chancers, factions, and snake-oil merchants, it had always been a relief to speak to Fennimore, to deal with that fairness, that clear, calm way of speaking, and to know you could rely on him to act in good faith.

"Want to know my guess?" Sigune said, and continued before I answered, "I think he did it to spike someone's guns. I can think of half-a-dozen grifters and shysters who think they could make a fortune as a border hosteller. I hope this Jessica wipes their eye."

"What have you been up to?" I asked, having left a sufficiently long pause to signal that I would change the subject. We had to find out first if this JQ had the skill, and then if she had the interest, and I could do without diplomats, even house-trained ones like Sigune, breathing down my neck.

"A bit of this, a bit of that," she said, helping herself to toast. "You heard about my falling out with the Huntmaster."

"The Hunt has to be in perfect fettle, you know that," I said, passing the cruet of raspberry jam to her. "Not every pup makes the sky-pack."

"I know! But the Huntmaster should not abandon the others! It's heartless!"

She crunched morosely on her toast. Sigune's other 'job', self-chosen and frankly illicit, is finding homes for the hounds of the sídhe who are rejected from the kennels of the Wild Hunt.

"I believe there is another of our East Lintzfield colleagues here," she said, surprising me. But then of course, she had signed the emergency pass so that Theo Solaita could use the Ambassadorial portals between Northumbria and Corrbofinn. "I hope she is not one of the troublemakers."

"She's not one of the diplomats, so we can hope. She's a translator, I believe."

"It might be worth checking her out," she said, sucking jammy crumbs off her claws, "just to be sure to be sure."

"There's something else I wanted to ask you. Were there any emergency passes that I didn't know about requested on the night of the killing?"

Sigune paused with one pincer still between her lips.

"Ah," she said, putting two and two together, "you counted the bells."

Later in the afternoon, I felt I had advanced some small way in my attempts to direct blame for the murder away from myself. I was not short of suspects: Niamh Bracken was just as likely as Angry Ponytail or Collier to be the person Delia should have suspected. Niamh was a property developer, she wanted Herne's Acre, she had had an altercation with Millar. Maybe what Delia had overheard was that Niamh owed money to, or was owed money by, Millar.

I decided I had earned a tea-break, maybe even a biscuit, and as I stood up to stretch, my phone rang. I had that horrible sort of jolt, like an electrical charge to the pit of the stomach, when I recognised the number. It was my work-place. My boss was calling me. My boss, calling me again on a Sunday; my boss who seemed to think that my time was his own.

My former boss, as of that moment.

The first thing I did, over the obligatory mug of tea and shock-absorbing biscuit, was to send an email to my brother, Brendan. Ostensibly, this was because he was helping me find a flat, and needed to know what rent I could afford. Mostly, though, I just felt better telling Brendan. Our younger brother Gerard would insult him with *bossy* when they fought as children, but Brendan is just very capable. This no longer annoys Gerard, and Olive, the baby, always took Brendan's sterling advice as her own personal entitlement. I did not expect him to find me another job, but Brendan and I are close, and his appearance on my troubled horizons was always like seeing the cavalry arrive.

I scoured the internet's job-market. I was struck by the chilling thought that I might now be condemned to the same sort of job as I had done in Past Designs. I would rather eat my own feet. The happy thought did strike me that as I no longer lived in Kirkaller, I could go anywhere. I liked Newcastle upon Tyne, but jobs weren't plentiful. London—rent could be insane, apart from those areas where I didn't want to live because… well, I wanted to live. Durham had a mediaeval cathedral and a botanic gardens, maybe a job lurked there. There was Glasgow, or Edinburgh, there was Cardiff. *Torchwood*, with Gwen's namesake, was shot in Cardiff. But were there jobs?

Within the hour, I had received a reply from Brendan saying *sack your guardian angel*, and even that cheered me up. I noticed a new email with the subject of *house-sale?* but before I could open it, I was startled by a knocking on the door. There was another surprise on the doorstep in the form of Butler and Birhanu. I invited them in, and immediately, Butler reached into her pocket.

"Recognise her?"

I glanced at the photograph, but shook my head. Whoever she was, she had curly brown hair, green eyes, and freckles sprayed all over a very round face. This, it seemed, was Gemma Broderick, Millar's irate ex-girlfriend.

"She came to see us as soon as she heard about Millar's death," Butler said. "Gemma was friendly with one Bridget Earley."

She paused, and Birhanu chipped in, "Gemma said they had arranged to meet at the party, but Bridget never showed up."

Again, there was a pause, and again I waited. I presumed they had a point they intended to get to.

"Might you have misheard Sorley?" Butler went on, "Might Bridget Earley have been the woman you spoke to as you arrived?"

I nodded and shrugged. They were both looking very solemn, and it made me uneasy.

"You spoke to her," Birhanu said, "yet no-one else mentions seeing her at all."

Butler said, looking directly at me for the first time, "There seems to me a possible reason why you are the only person who saw Bridget Earley at that party."

"The reason being?"

Butler did not answer, but continued looking at me, as if she was waiting for me to catch on. I glanced at Birhanu and saw him watching me too, without expression.

"Oh, for the love of God!" I suddenly understood. "You think I am Bridget Earley!"

Neither detective answered me, but they both shifted their positions slightly, tilted their heads.

"You think I came all this distance to prance about in high heels and a stupid banshee outfit, spying on what's his name at the cottage—"

"Coll—" Birhanu stopped himself, but not before Butler glared at him. *Aha*, I thought. *Ivo Collier.*

"Well, good luck to you proving it." I was startled at my own rebarbative tone. First Louise. Then my employer. Now this.

"I'm sure you have a passport," Butler said.

"I do, Inspector," I snapped, "but have you any right to demand to see it?"

"You could just show it to me," she said, her words more agreeable than her tone, "get us out of your hair."

"You could just get out of my hair by getting out of my

house." I felt weirdly reckless. I really had no idea what auth-ority the guards *did* have, but I was clearly in the humour to take my chances. "The door is just there."

Butler continued to eye me beadily for a few seconds, and then she nodded, and left, Birhanu in her wake.

Eight

ALONE, I WAS TOO distracted to continue my job-search. I felt shaky. Even if I was not sure that they suspected me of murder, I did not know how to react to their bizarre suspicion that I had come to the party disguised as Bridget Earley. Besides, I had not yet recovered from the shock of losing my job. I filled the kettle again.

Waiting for it to boil, I fretted over money. I had some savings despite dipping into them as utility bills went up but Louise's taste for city-breaks did not diminish; she earned more as a hotel manager than I did as the Support Services Officer in the Pit of Hell—sorry, in Past Designs, "the leader in heritage-industry reproduction services and exhibition management." On the other hand, I did not know how much Herne's Acre would fetch, but I had at least one interested buyer in Niamh Bracken. Maybe I would regain some luck, and find a job I actually liked, maybe in a museum again. My dream job.

Well, not exactly my dream job, no, my dream job was unrealistic, and whatever mistakes I may have made, I have always been realistic. Practical. I would get a grip on what needed to be done. But first I would try and enjoy the thought that I would soon have no responsibility for soothing the tempers of callers to Support Services, negotiating the ego of my boss and his lackeys, or working out which of our over-burdened, under-staffed resources had sprung a leak.

I went upstairs. It was after half-four now, and dark. I switched on the lights in the office, and sat down at my laptop. Contrary to my expectations, the email saying *house sale?* was not from Niamh. It was from someone called Regan O'Moore.

It was a very clear, polite email. Familiar with Hen Rosse's herbal courses, it seems, Regan O'Moore was now interested in obtaining Herne's Acre to set up in a similar business herself. Could I let her know the likely sale price, and could she come and see it?

Well, that was encouraging. Two people interested, and the place wasn't even on the market. I had no idea about a price, but I would find an estate agent. I scrolled down to the bottom of Regan's email and found her signature-block. *Koré's World. Beautiful Things for Beautiful You.* The email had only been sent an hour ago, and it was nearly five on a Sunday. I would perform my first tiny act of freedom and ignore a business-related email until an actual working day. I'm such a rebel.

Getting up from the desk, I glanced first at my attempt to plot out who might have killed Tony Millar, but somehow the news of my job-loss made murder less worrying. That train of thought reminded me that Birhanu had let slip the information that Collier had been the person seen snooping about Delia's cottage. I recalled at the party, Collier smoothing his damp hair. I turned to go. I needed to see if I had enough in the house to make dinner, or if I would have to haul Gwen out of her cosy garage and go shopping.

As I passed the table onto which I had moved the plan of the Carnsore Glasshouse, I stopped dead, so abruptly that I stumbled. I knew for a certainty that I had left all Hen Rosse's hand-drawn plans in a pile, and that the table had been clear except for a few folders, and a large book, bound in leather and marbled green paper, with *Poison* embossed in dark gold. Now, the table was covered with the plans laid out in order to show the whole field.

Everything looked beautiful. Carnsore, Rockall, Fair Isle glasshouses I had already noticed; the poison garden had Fastnet. The field was divided up into gardens, and the maritime theme continued there, with Tyne, Wight, Cromarty. I did not know which was more disconcerting: the fact that the plans were arranged differently from how I had left them, or that they so resembled a physic garden I dreamed of creating.

I walked away quickly. I could not afford dreams, certainly not now. Downstairs I checked the fridge and the press, opening the doors very firmly, firmly noting what was available for dinner, firmly writing a list of things I needed. Gwen could stand down, since I had the ingredients for dinner, and I expressed my resolution to be practical and realistic by firmly preparing dinner. I even ate a biscuit with determination. The fear that I would run amok and refuse to get a proper job waned over the evening. After dinner— a very sensible and very hot curry of chickpeas and potatoes —and dishes, I went into Hen's library. I found the run of Dorothy L. Sayers in cloth-covered hardback. Pondering briefly on the fact that, if Golden Age detection is to be believed, the British upper classes are a scandalously murderous and venal crew, I selected *Have His Carcase*, and settled in for the evening.

Once in bed, sleep seemed reluctant to visit. I had just begun to worry that I would be awake all night when I did fall asleep, but not just to sleep, I fell into dreaming; not just to dreaming, but to dreamwalking.

I was on a path between Herne's Acre and the Heathcote lands. Someone else was at the far end of the path, a broad-shouldered figure in a tightly-cut coat. The figure was tall, but the bulk looked soft to me. It was standing with its hands in its pockets, but I could not see the face. There were two other figures, one on each side. Between me and the three visitors, there was a dog, a mere pup, something like a Dobermann but white with red ears. It was pacing nervously, its back legs crouched, and its tail tucked tightly between them. I was dressed, which was a blessing.

It was a peculiar moment, when I knew exactly where and who I was and yet nothing seemed familiar: the sky was dark emerald and the stars looked red, the moon was blue, I could smell every single plant, every wildflower, every decayed berry, every plant in the poison garden, but instead of being overwhelmed I felt invigorated. I had come to consciousness in this world only a few seconds, when the figure in the tight coat snapped its fingers, and a nasal voice ordered *get it*. The two men ran forward and the pup, realising the threat, ran straight to me. Without thinking, I stepped in front of it.

The men kept running, pelting toward me like they were spring-heeled. I yelled at them,

"This is Herne's Acre! You are trespassing. Get out and stay out!"

The pup was looking at me admiringly. *I* was looking at me admiringly. The men continued running, taking much longer to reach me than was really possible; the field behind my house wasn't *that* big. I felt the ground tremble, but not just from the running feet, and without any idea of what I was doing, I threw out my arms and before we knew where we were, the running men had crashed into a hedge of hornbeams that had not been there a moment before. With equal abruptness, I was standing out at the edge of the field, beside the willow trees, the red-eared pup beside me, looking up at me.

"Alright, Fido," I said, and it jerked its chin at me with an indignant air, "come along."

Thornapple's Narrative. Commission Headquarters Monday 24th October.

I marched into Sigune's office.

"What were you *thinking?*"

Sigune looked shifty, but rallied. "Now, I know, I know, I know what you think," she said, holding up her claws in a placatory way, "but let me explain."

"You can't *do* that sort of thing," I said, closing the door quickly, knowing our juniors had their own gossip-economy. "You *invaded her dream.* You brought *a hound of the sídhe* over to the human side."

"It was in a good cause!" Sigune cried, but quietly, "in *two* good causes! Maybe even *three!*"

Sigune was a diplomat, accustomed to the world of double-speak and oblique expression, but she usually was straight-forward with me. I sat down and waited.

"I admit," she said, luring me to acceptance of what was to come by acknowledging fault, "that I invaded her dream so as to get the pup to safety. But!"

Sigune moves fast for a big being, and she seemed to barely have hopped out of her seat before we both had steaming mugs before us. The aroma was ambrosial, and for good reason.

"Clearly this human is a dream-walker," Sigune went on,

"and therefore *could* act as Hosteller for us at Herne's Acre, something we all want. Not just us, but the loss of a hostel always brings a decline to the area, so we will be doing everyone—Heathcote, the village, Lissascaul—everyone, a favour."

"Accepted," I was grudging.

"She has a house. Fennimore made some financial provision too. The dog is an additional tie. But that's only the *maybe* good cause. I found something out for you."

She leaned her linen-sleeved elbows on her desk.

"You've been plagued by trespassers," she said, "I've heard about all the complaints."

"I cannot work it out," I admitted. "Unfortunate Cray thinks they might be using an old track, but—"

"Cray is right," Sigune sat back triumphantly. "You couldn't find it because it is not of the usual sort."

"What is it?"

"A bridle-path."

"I never even *thought* of that!"

"No reason why you should," Sigune sounded pleased with herself. "We thought they were all gone. But I went looking, and when your JQ went dream-walking, I got the pup from… where I had hidden it, and I let it go. With a pup from the Wild Hunt Kennels on it, I could see the track clearly, and also saw that where Herne's Acre meets the road to Cotter's Hill, the bridle track has become visible. Humans can cross it."

"Are you sure?"

"That's how I was able to get the pup to the human side. And there were three toughs there, too. Your JQ sent them packing. I bet some human has been using that crossing-point to get to the sídhe. I don't know what for."

I could imagine what for. Humans are a rum crew when it comes to risk. What I didn't know was *who*.

"I have something else for you," she said, with an air of having just recalled it, though I suspected she had kept this something up her sleeve either to charm me back into good temper or reward me for being peaceable. "I know who the extra visitor was on the night of the killing."

This was good news. Each time the Sídhe cross to the mortal side, my sídhe-side co-workers send over copies of the passes they had signed, and I count the peals of the Border Bell to see that the numbers matched. On the night of Millar's death, there had been three passes, but four peals of the bells. If someone from the Other Side was up to mischief at Cotter's Lodge, the sooner we knew, the better.

"Do you know Elcmar Cecht?" Sigune told me.

I didn't, but Cecht was a well-known name among antique and art dealers on the Other Side, so I took a punt that Elcmar was one of these. Sigune nodded.

"He gave his visiting address as Killmore House, and reason for visit was business."

"That's the new residence for the Representative from the Isle of Apples, isn't it? Over near Killmorbawn? It's being renovated…"

"All in the hands of Ivo Collier."

"That is some feather in his cap," I said. Sigune was smiling, clearly anticipating my catching up with her conclusion. "Ooooh—Millar was one of Collier's suppliers," I spoke as I realised, "and Collier would be in deep, deep doo-doo if anything for *that* residence was not up to snuff."

"It's more than quality he has to worry about," Sigune crossed her knife and fork on her plate to indicate to the canteen staff she was finished; it always made me flinch because where I'm from, it is an invitation to an argument. "It's safety. Everyone knows the drill: only mortals step on mortal ground. The rest of us have to be careful about all sorts of things: mirrors, bells, doors, pottery. If the wrong thing turned out to be mortal-made and not sídhe-stuff— well. Makes you wonder why Collier needed advice so late in the day from Cecht, and why Cecht was so willing to come running."

I said nothing. We left together, and I took the long way back to my office. Collier had given Millar a public dressing-down for skimping on the quality of his supplies, for fiddling his prices. Could Millar have taken a potentially catastrophic revenge? Supplied something that Collier as a matter of urgency suddenly sought advice about from an expert on sídhe-goods?

Nine

Jessica Quill's Narrative. Herne's Acre Monday 24th October.

THE NIGHT'S ADVENTURES had worn me out and I slept until the morning was bright. I always remember my dream-walks, and I had a little thrill of pleasure at recalling how effective and firm I had been in my dream last night, seeing unknown miscreants off my property. Pulling on my slippers, and fumbling for a dressing-gown, I wondered what happened to dream-dogs.

Apparently, some dream-dogs come back with you, sleep on your furniture, and piddle on your floor. I stood in my kitchen, goggling in bewilderment at the white, claret-eared pup that sat beside my settee, looking rather sheepishly at a puddle near the back door. He barked softly, with a definitely hopeful note.

"Really?" I said aloud, and the hound put his head on one side. I approached him—a little gingerly, he was a pretty big animal for all he was a pup—and he began to thump his tail against the edge of the settee. I held out my hand: he thrust his snout into the palm, and then licked it very thoroughly. My mind was a blank, I had no idea how to work out what had happened, but the animal was very much there, so I needed to deal with his presence.

"What am I even to call you?" I said to him, glancing at his collar-less neck. The puppy made a strange sort of elongated, undulating sound, somewhere between a whine and a squeak.

"Pupsqueak, then," I said, and I tell no lie, the puppy rolled its eyes.

"What will we feed you?" I asked, and Pupsqueak bounded to his feet. I had no dogfood, so I cobbled together a meal of oats and eggs, which he snarfed with enthusiasm.

Then I shooed him outside while I stumbled about making tea and toast.

Rather than start the day looking for a job I needed but did not want, I went out after breakfast to collect the herbs that Molly Thompson had asked for. Hen Rosse's plans guided me to the Rockall glasshouse to get the peppermint and to shake some seeds from the fennel plant, still beautiful in October, but I had to go as far as Forties for the aniseed and lemon balm. Walking back to the house as the misty rain was clearing, I called Molly's phone-number.

The number you have dialled is not available.

I tried it again, and got the same message. For a moment, I was dismayed. Back in the house, I checked my notebook, where I had put the slip on which Molly had written down the number. I had entered it correctly in my phone. I supposed her phone might have been damaged. I could ring Dermot.

My eye fell on an adjacent page. There was a list of phone numbers in my own writing. The list of phone numbers I had taken from Millar's phone. I looked from one to the other. I looked out of the back door window, without seeing the lavender rain-haze blotting out the trees at Heathcote, and calling to mind instead Molly leaving my house, saying that she had not known Millar. And her phone-number had been in his phone.

My mind was blank for a few seconds, then a dozen thoughts came crowding in. Molly had lied about knowing Millar. Did she have a motive to kill him? Was she another girlfriend? Unwilling to accept his infidelities? As a motive, it seemed unlikely. If Delia was anything to go by, I could not really see Millar hitting on someone who dressed like a 1980s highwayman and expected me to drop everything to respond to her request for herbs.

I went to my plan of the murder, and added Molly's name. I had not seen her at the party, but then, several people were in disguise—unless there had been *real* banshees, witches, and goblins there. I looked at Hen Rosse's plans, laid out but not as I left them. I thought about the website that disappeared. I heard the pup barking outside.

Putting aside banshees, I rang Dermot, and asked if he had his sister's new phone number. He was surprised to hear that Molly had changed her phone, but gave me her address. I scribbled it down and, as I have never been able to follow spoken directions, also scribbled a hasty map. I backed Gwen out of the garage, and then looked at the dog looking at me. I really would have to bring it to a dog-shelter, but in the meantime...

Molly lived about a mile and a half east of Herne's Acre, on the road to Tuarashee. Hers was a new-looking house, and the small garden and the roadside hedge all had a raw air to them. The house was looped by a gravel path through patchy new lawn. I parked in front of the door, and let Pup-squeak out, bidding him keep Gwen company.

I wondered if the house had been built on the site of an older one, because behind it was a row of four small sheds that looked considerably older, though their conversion to kennels looked recent. There were some trees not far off, complete with rookery, the sounds of cows in the distance, and of dogs close by. Pupsqueak barked in reply.

Molly was surprised to see me, and looked frankly scared when I said I had been unable to contact her by phone. She had abandoned her highwayman look, and today she looked like an advertisement for someone's autumn collection, all rich colours, chestnut-curls wig, and smoky eyeshadow.

"Sorry," she said, and her lip gloss shimmered like wet hawberries as she smiled, "I dropped the phone and smashed it. I'm still getting my contacts list back in order. You're very good to bring the herbs here. Can I get you a cup of tea or something?"

I accepted the tea, and a tiny tightening of her shoulders suggested she had been hoping I would just go away. Molly did not attempt to make small talk while she filled the kettle, and I wavered between trying to lure information out of her and just asking her directly. I decided on the latter.

"Terrible thing about Millar," I said. "Was he a close friend of yours?"

"I told you before, I didn't know him."

"He had your telephone number in his phone," I said. The look she gave me over her shoulder was dreadful. All she said was,

"What makes you think that?"

"I had his phone accidentally, and I saw the numbers he had stored."

Her mouth moved in a sort of repressed spasm, and after a few seconds she said very calmly,

"I did not. You must have made a mistake."

"Well, I suppose the police will check it out, I gave the phone to them. They'll start ringing around."

"I expect so."

"Unless, of course, someone broke their—"

"These things happen," she snapped.

Clearly, Molly intended to stick to denial, so there did not seem much else I could say. The fact that she was so anxious, and was lying about it, pointed strongly to there being something illegal or at least illicit to hide. Did she have something to do with his death? These 'boosters' I did not quite understand?

"Sorry," Molly said, "I had nothing to do with his death, I don't want anyone thinking otherwise."

"If it makes you feel better, Delia Fitzgerald blames me. She thinks he and I had some row over my house, over Herne's Acre. I never met the man before the party, let alone had a row with him."

"He was poisoned, wasn't he?" Now that we were not talking about her, Molly's colour had come back. "Dermot told me that the coroner's report—"

"Already?" I was astonished. "I thought that took weeks."

Molly looked alarmed again.

"Around here," she said, and started again, "I mean… it depends. I think. But he definitely was poisoned. Difficult thing to give someone at a party."

"I think they think it might have been in—is it *boosters* they're called?"

The kettle boiled, and while she made the tea, I watched through the glass of her back door a stout cocker spaniel waddling past the sheds. Molly changed the subject from murder, and asked me about where I lived in England. She had spent a summer working in the Midland Hotel in Morecambe, and we exchanged anecdotes, as I had once gone on holiday there. I finished my tea, and feeling that sufficiently friendly relations had been established, I asked as I got up,

"Do you know anyone who worked with Millar? There was someone at the party, with a ponytail, if I could find her, I might shake the guards' suspicion of me."

"I'm sure they don't suspect you," she said, kindly rather than convincingly. "I don't know any of his contacts, no."

I thanked her, and Molly walked me to the door. I had parked Gwen facing away from the house, and when I went outside, Pupsqueak was standing by the car, looking at us. I turned to ask Molly if she knew of a dog shelter, but to my astonishment, she was staring at the dog. She looked sick, so pale she was nearly green. Before I could say a word, she stepped back into the house and slammed the door. I was very thoughtful on my way home.

Not having had a dog when I arrived, and not knowing for how long I would have this one, I had no food for Pupsqueak. As soon as I put Gwen in the garage, I hunted for something that would suffice as a leash until I was able to buy a proper one. It was a short hunt because as soon as I went into the utility room, I found a very fine green leather collar and leash hanging on the back of the door. This was getting silly. It felt like Herne's Acre was putting things into my hands. I introduced Pupsqueak to the leash, and we set off for Pallasalee.

Pallasalee was a neat village, strung along on either side of a beech-thatched green where the road to Heathcote peeled away from the main road from Lissascaul across the county border to Drumkyle. There was a post office and general grocer's shop, two pubs, a tiny café-cum-bookshop, a dozen and a half houses, and an undertaker's. The corvids that lived on the green were making a great racket as I approached, a tattered cloud of them circling overhead and gradually descending to settle on the winter-bald round crowns of the beeches.

As I crossed the road to the shop, I heard my name being called, and saw Dermot beckoning to me. Jamie Conyngham was with him, and Ivo Collier.

"We were just about to get lunch," Dermot said, "join us. There's someone for you to meet—Millar's ex-wife."

He dropped his voice. "We heard that Delia's blaming you, and you never know, Theo might be able to tell you something that would help the investigation along."

"I just need to get some food for the dog," I said, and Dermot said immediately,

"Bring it in, Coll Whalen's a demon for dogs. He'll feed it."

Ivo was looking marginally less exotic than he had at Delia's party, but very sharp, very Peak Sinatra. Jamie was relaxed in a lumberjack shirt and black jeans.

"I believe you were the means of Millar's body being discovered," Ivo smiled at me.

"I was. I fell over his feet."

"I can't believe I had left before the excitement started," Ivo said. "I don't wish to be tasteless, of course. Though Millar was a bit of a tick."

"How well did you know him?"

Ivo looked directly at me, and smiled, but Dermot was ushering us in, saying with a showman's air,

"Jessica, meet Theo Solaita."

"Hello, Theo Solaita," I said approaching the table, "how are you?"

"Areet, marra," Theo Solaita said, holding out a slim hand, which I shook.

"Areet, bonny lass?" I replied, in probably the worst Geordie accent ever. Theo tipped her head back and laughed. She wore black trousers, and a thin wool shirt striped in rich colours; in true Northern style, she had no jacket or jumper despite the cold. Her hair was curled and shoulder-length, and held back in a loose pony-tail.

"I work in Newcastle," I explained. "Worked. In Past Designs, do you know it?"

Theo accepted a pint of Guinness while she thought. "On Pilgrim Street—or no, Shakespeare Street? You do reproductions of artwork for, like, theatres and exhibitions?"

"That's us. I was service support. What do you do, yourself?"

Theo darted a very quick glance at Dermot, who was handing menus out. "I'm in the civil service. I'm a translator."

Ten

To keep off the subject of my job, I asked Theo about hers. Though I had some difficulty in understanding exactly for whom she worked or to what end, I did understand that it involved translating official and bureaucratic documents into Spanish or French and occasionally, though here she became more than a little vague, some minority languages too.

"I hear you fell over the corpse of my ex-husband," she said, and I offered awkward condolences.

"It's alright. It's a shock alright, but it was all a long time ago."

"How long were you married?"

"Nearly three years."

The landlord came over to take our orders. I recognised him from Delia's party, he had managed the bar. He was a tall, long-armed man, clean-shaven and with very short hair, entirely white although he did not look particularly old.

As Dermot had predicted, proceedings stopped while Whalen lavished attention on Pupsqueak. We gave our orders, but the first food brought out was a plate of chopped liver with egg and biscuit for the dog.

"What exactly happened?" Theo asked, "I was talking to your police—what do you call them?"

"The guards," Dermot said. "Properly, it's Gardaí—the Garda Síochána are 'the guardians of the peace'—but 'guards' will do."

"Well, they wouldn't really tell me anything. Investigation ongoing, they said."

Theo asked the same kinds of questions that the guards had asked all of us at different points, and each one of us chipped in with an answer. When Ivo described the fight with Gemma, Theo demanded,

"Is that our answer? A fight? Then a murder? Shortest episode of *Midsomer Murders* ever?"

"I don't think it could be. Gemma was gone a couple of hours before he died. Atropine acts faster than that."

"You know about poisons?" Theo asked.

"I used to work in a museum of medical plants. Lots of plants that are poisonous are also medicinal. Atropine is used during surgery, because it inhibits saliva, so you don't choke on spit when you're anaesthetised. You can use atropine to treat poisoning by some nerve agents, too, even sarin."

"Really?" Dermot sounded almost disbelieving. "I thought sarin killed you dead immediately."

"You've up to ten minutes. Depends on how much sarin you've ingested."

"Does it take much atropine to kill a person?"

"Well, with all poisons it depends," I said, beginning to wonder if it was such a good idea to sound like an expert on how to commit murder in the way that a murder had recently been committed, "depends on the size of the person, age, health, lots of things. It's very chancy. Also, atropine is very bitter, foul-tasting. If the killer was relying on feeding it to Millar, they'd have to make sure it was in something like, say, coffee."

"I don't think Millar was drinking coffee," Jamie sounded emphatic. "Nothing that wasn't at least eighty proof passed his lips all evening, I'd say."

"What kind of a plant is atropine?" Ivo asked, almost cutting across Dermot. "What family, like?"

"Solanaceae."

"Aren't tomatoes Solanaceae?" Theo said, "Bell peppers? They're not poisonous."

"No. Well, very unripe tomatoes are, a bit," I said, recalling the unpleasant consequences of a green tomato curry I had once tried, "they have tomatine. Tomato leaves have solanine, not atropine, but they're the same family as belladonna. Deadly nightshade."

Silence descended while Whalen brought the food, and then I said,

"How is Delia, Jamie?"

He made a face, doubtful but hopeful.

"She seems to be getting better," he said, and then said to Theo,

"Apparently, Tony was using boosters—"

"No!" said Ivo, and at the same time Theo said,

"Bloody little monkey-hanger!"

With one part of my mind, I tried to dredge up who the insult of *monkey-hanger* was used against, but with the other part, I put two and two together. Ivo, with his own weirdly blue eyes, and his current look of horror and alarm.

"He was getting the boosters from you, Ivo," I said. He jerked his head towards me, and didn't answer. The awkward silence stretched on. Ivo looked at Jamie, then at me, then at Jamie.

"I gave him some," he admitted, "not regularly. Only if I had extra, if he was stuck. I didn't think—"

"Do you know who else supplied him?"

Ivo was so self-possessed, he would have probably dodged the question if he had not been wrong-footed by realising

that he had inadvertently helped Millar manipulate Delia.
"No—"

"There was a woman at the party," I pressed further,
"about Millar's height, ponytail, in outdoor clothes. She was
warning Millar not to tell anyone about something she had
sold—was that to do with buildings? Renovations?"

"*That* was why—"

Ivo cut across Jamie, saying, "I didn't see anyone in outdoor
clothes."

I tend to be a bit of a Labrador about people, and assume
they are truthful. But there was something about the way
Ivo answered me, the particularity of the *in outdoor clothes*
that made me certain he was lying. Disguise, then? Angry
Ponytail had not been in disguise when I saw her. Could she
have gone away and come back?

"You wouldn't do us a favour, would you?" Theo said to
me, breaking the tense silence. "The, ah, guards asked me
to go up to Tony's house. I'm not sure what they expect me
to find, they said *just anything unusual*. It'd be nice to have
a friendly face there. I was thinking, Wednesday."

At first, I calculated quickly in my head—did I have time
before my ten days' leave was up—but with a rush of liber-
ated joy, I recollected my ex-boss. I said I would be delighted.

*'The Nook,' Firgloss Road, Pettimills. Wednesday 26th
October.*

I met Theo at Millar's house.. Millar had lived on the near
side of Pettimills. Just before the roundabout going into the
town, I turned off to the right and up a rather battered driveway, and when I got to the top, Theo was leaning against
the boot of her car, waiting.

It was a bright day, and mild for the time of year, though there was the threat of rain on the light wind. Millar's house was big and new, with a neat if unimaginative garden front and back, and a boundary hedge of hazel and what looked like leylandii. I was very surprised to see, along the right-hand side of the back garden, half-hidden in rhododendrons, the charred remains of some structure, something made of wood and metal mesh. The wood that was not burned looked new.

"What on earth happened?"

Theo came to stand beside me. "I don't know, apart from the obvious. Tony had dogs the time I was here, but why anyone would have set kennels on fire, I don't know."

"What kind of dogs?" I asked. The burned remains looked like the structure, whatever it had been, had been very small. I walked a little closer, squatting down to peer in through the heat-twisted mesh.

"I don't know—he had two dogs in the house when I was there, he was finishing up getting their paperwork from a chap when I arrived. One was a boxer, she was young-looking. The other was a Labrador. I don't know if he had others."

"Come on," I said, puzzled. "Let's have a look inside the house."

Whatever 'entrepreneur' might mean, it seemed to pay well. The house had two storeys and a steeply pitched roof, with an all-glass extension on one side. Inside, everything was open-plan with lots of glass; prosaic mind that I have, I wondered about the cost of cleaning guano off so much glass since presumably birds lived in the trees behind the house.

It seemed an overwhelmingly cluttered space, not the amount of furniture as much as the fussy patterns and bright colours. The office at the back of the house could have been lovely, as it looked out over the back garden that dipped so the view went right the way across to the Slate Hills. But the garish carpet and the vividly floral curtains would not have given me a moment's rest.

We went, Theo and I, methodically through each room. Millar's house had been picked over by the guards, and it showed. The only room that yielded anything of interest was the office—study, I suppose I should call it, considering the bookshelves. Theo said there had been papers over the desk and chair, and on the floor, that the guards had taken. I kept my hands in my pockets, as there was no need to give the guards any more reason for suspecting me, but I looked carefully at what was left.

"I'm not sure what the, the, the guards think I might notice," Theo said anxiously. "I hadn't known Tony in years, I don't know what to expect."

I looked over her shoulder at the shelf of CDs and DVDs. There were some compilations of power ballads and rom-coms that seemed out of place amongst the Springsteen back catalogue and the action-thriller blockbusters. I wondered if these romantic intrusions were the residue of girlfriends, and then wondered if I was being sexist.

"Anything that *is* here strike you as unusual?"

Theo looked around a bit helplessly.

"No. I mean, when I was here before I was surprised about the dogs, he'd never wanted one. I did. But then we lived in a city, maybe in the countryside it was different. He might have wanted a guard dog. A boxer would be good."

"Theo, what kind of music did Millar enjoy?" I had moved

over to the bookshelf. Some of the space was filled with full sets in green leather of untouched copies of Dickens and Shakespeare. The books showing signs of use were either biographies of sports or Irish historical figures, or else were by Robert Ludlum or Michael Crichton. Theo shook her head.

"I don't know. Whatever was popular. Whatever was on the radio."

"You wouldn't expect him to have a biography of Wagner, then?"

Theo came to join me. "I don't think he listened to a bar of Wagner in his life."

I might be a philistine, though I did give *The Ring Cycle* a whirl, but I can't say I blamed him. The large volume of *Richard Wagner: A Life* stood out amongst things like *The Bourne Supremacy* and *The Lions of Lucerne*. I took off my scarf, and wrapped my hands in the cloth before picking up the book and putting it on the desk.

We flicked over the pages, and found nothing. Feeling like I was in a film, I stood it upright, and shone my phone-torch down the spine. Nothing. Then I laid it flat again, and opened first the front cover, and then the back.

"What—" I said, and Theo said, "There!"

The back cover was fatter than the front, as if it was padded. The corner of the endpaper had come away, and we had both seen another underlying it, in a different colour. It took only a slight tug to pull up the endpaper, and we saw that three or four sheets of paper had been tucked in. Theo hesitated, but I confess, I did not. I pulled the end-paper back further, enough to see the solicitor's headed notepaper, the date, and that the top paper was referring to Niamh Bracken.

"Butler will have your hide if she thinks you've been snooping," Theo said, and pulled the book away from me.

"But—"

"But they *asked* me to come here," she went on, coolly and neatly tugging out the papers, "they can't complain if I find something."

What she had found were letters between Millar and his solicitor, regarding his intention of suing Niamh Bracken for non-payment of work done. There was nothing as useful as details, but the fact that Millar had hidden the paperwork suggested unusual caution. Who might have come to his house and accidentally seen these? Hardly Niamh. Did he have a cleaner he didn't trust?

Theo put the papers back, and tucked the volume under her arm.

"Something to give to the police," she said. "Good. Butler has a look about her, makes you want to be helpful."

We parted company at the gate to Millar's house, Theo destined for Lissascaul to hand over what we had found to Butler and Birhanu, and Gwen and I returning to Herne's Acre.

Eleven

Herne's Acre, Wednesday 26th October.

MY INTENTION WAS to sensibly spend time looking for a new job, but I promised myself I would face into that dreary duty just as soon as I did a little checking on the internet. However peculiarly the Corrbofinn website behaved, surely individual businesses had normal ways of advertising themselves, and maybe some link with Millar might be revealed.

But I had underestimated the level to which businesses in rural areas could successfully rely on word-of-mouth rather than anything more pushy. Collier was the only one who had a formal website, and even at that, the links refused to open. Unable to quite face the job search, I went to Regan O'Moore's email, and opened the link to Koré's World.

The website was terribly stylish, and all very lovely, and in an odd way terribly familiar, although I would never have had reason to buy anything from it. Their designer had chosen a cracking palette, very rich and autumnal, everything looking highly polished but not crassly shiny. It managed to give the impression that all of this really would make your life better, even something called a face-roller, which made me laugh, thinking of people rolling themselves out anew, like gingerbread men. I clicked on the 'Meet Our Team' link to photographs and biographies.

Regan O'Moore had a wide face and a long, full mouth, that curled up a little at each end, even in repose. She had amber-brown eyes and a definitely mischievous look. Her hair was cut to her jawline, and she wore Celtic knot earrings. My eye slid over the photographs and mini-biographies of Kore's other founders and directors, and to my astonishment, I saw someone I recognised.

Patricia Hopkins had dark-blue eyes, and she wore a sapphire-coloured top that made both her hair and eyes shine. She had vibrantly blonde hair, like ripe corn, twisted sleekly up her head, unlike the last time I had seen her, when her hair had been swinging angrily behind her while she threatened to cut Tony Millar's throat.

I enlarged the photo and looked again. Was I absolutely sure? My instinct was *yes*, but was I right? The hallway had been dim, I had not seen her well enough to describe her to anyone. But her build, her profile, looked right.

In the brief few lines under her photograph, she mentioned her work on renovation and restoration, which meant my guess had been right, she was in the same professional world as Collier, so precise about saying he had seen "no-one in outdoor clothes." Was this a connection? Did he think she was involved? Or did he owe her a favour? Was it just Hopkins? Or anyone else in Koré's World?

While I was pondering the possibilities, my phone rang. It was Karolina, inviting me to lunch at Cotter's Lodge.

"Delia is better, but is very embarrassed. Come and say you forgive her for accusing you of murder."

Karolina managed to make it all sound a bit of a lark, which amused me, so I agreed. While I scrubbed my hair in the en-suite's tiny shower, I kept picking away at the idea that I had identified Angry Ponytail. By the time I was dried and dressed, I realised that while I was sure, I was not sure enough to go to the guards and give them her name. Her initials had not been on Millar's phone either. There had been a TH, not PH, and no-one else had seen her at the party, either.

Cotter's Lodge, Wednesday 26th October.
Delia was certainly much less mimosa-like at lunch. She had lost her limp and clingy air, and had exchanged her crushed velvet and ribbons for moss-green trousers and a claret-coloured top with a pale floral design. The house was empty of SOCOs, and the lunch laid out in the conservatory. Lorcan saw Pupsqueak in the back of Gwen and insisted that four-legged guests were as welcome as the two-legged, and rustled up a couple of dog-biscuits, not a crumb of which Pupsqueak left behind. Only after we had eaten, and Lorcan had put on some coffee, did Delia bring up the question of Millar.

"I know Mam told you about the boosters," she sighed as she spoke, as one facing up to an unpleasant topic, "and I just wanted to apologise for, you know…"

"Telling the guards Jemima here had murdered your boyfriend!" Lorcan was not letting her off lightly.

"Yes, that," Delia said. "It's Jessica, Da; sorry, he can never get names right."

I recalled he had introduced me to other guests as "Hannah? Martina?"

"That's alright. But why? I mean, was it a random accusation, or did you have a reason…?"

She sighed heavily again. "It's horrible having to remember yourself acting like such a muppet."

"Don't insult muppets," Lorcan pounced, and Karolina said,

"Welcome to adulting, pet."

"It wasn't entirely random," Delia said to me. "Tony had a lot of business interests. He called himself an entrepreneur. I never really knew what he meant, but he would never explain."

"That's an egotist for you," her mother remarked, "always has to be the only one who knows the full story."

"But I would hear bits of conversations," Delia went on, "if I was in his house and someone called. There was something to do with Herne's Acre. He was always very *oh, don't trouble your pretty head*, so I didn't know much. But someone owed him money for some work he had done on Herne's Acre."

Oh-oh-oh, I thought immediately. Millar's hidden papers, about 'work completed', and Niamh Bracken not paying him for it.

"In fairness, I can see why you thought it was me," I said. "What kind of work? Building work?"

"I assumed so," Delia shook her head, "I know he said he had pulled in a lot of favours to make it look good—convincing. And another time he said *you're the niece, sell.* Though—no, he couldn't have, could he? If you never spoke to him."

"Might he have said to someone else to *get* the niece to sell?" Karolina asked, and then said to me, "Anyone been pressuring you to sell?"

Niamh was the first person to spring to mind. Regan O'Moore. But Regan was hardly pressuring, it was a polite enquiry. Though she worked with Patricia Hopkins—if Hopkins was Angry Ponytail, maybe O'Moore was in renovations too? But if Niamh could afford to buy my house, she could afford to pay Millar, surely. Unless—Hen Rosse had run a business based on what she grew at Herne's Acre.

Could it be that Niamh planned to do the same, and to pay Millar back from the profits? Millar became impatient?

"Ivo Collier wasn't on to you about it, no?" Lorcan said, and I glanced up at him, surprised. He darted a somewhat apologetic glance at Karo as he spoke. I shook my head. Delia sounded impatient as she said,

"Da thinks Ivo wants a piece of anything connected to—"

"The coffee must be ready, Lorcan," Karolina cut across Delia, and as Lorcan almost clumsily bounded to his feet, Karolina nudged Delia's foot sharply with her own. Connected with what? I wondered. What was at Herne's Acre that could interest a high-end renovation expert? When Lorcan returned with the coffee, he changed the conversation very firmly to plans for Christmas. What with everything that had happened, Delia's siblings were returning to Cotter's Lodge for the festive season as a show of support.

"The last time we were all together for Christmas was just after we bought this place," Lorcan said, and Karolina added,

"Well, the first Christmas it was still being fixed up. It was the one after that."

"Lorcan told me it was in bad shape when you bought it," I said, and Karolina rolled her eyes.

"The chap who owned it," she said, "he died when he was doing some home improvements, hit a live wire with his drill."

"Daddy checked under the plaster," Delia added, " found the wires were all over the place, complete cowboy job. The only wonder was that no-one had fried themselves before then."

"The great thing about all the kids together," Lorcan said, grinning at Karolina, "is that our eldest is a chef, and has promised to take care of the food."

I wondered where I would be at Christmas: probably each of my siblings would offer an invitation to join them, but I rather liked the idea of festive solitude. Not in the mangy little flat I was currently in, but somewhere.

When Pupsqueak and I returned to my house, I rang Dermot and left a message asking if Millar had worked on Herne's Acre. Then I turned my rather sleepy, post-prandial attention to finding a job and a home. There were a couple of jobs similar to the one I had just lost, and I shuddered as I read them. Having worked on that particular coal-face I could now correctly interpret the expectations behind phrases like "people-person," "adaptable," and "passionate." Brendan had sent me links to a couple of possible flats to live in, which looked lovely if you did not look at the expected rent, so I looked for jobs in Norwich and York. It was not an encouraging experience.

Late in the afternoon, Dermot called to the house.

"I got your message," he said, dragging off his beanie and giving Pupsqueak's ears a quick ruffle, "but as I was passing I thought I'd call."

Millar had not, Dermot was sure, been officially involved in any way with Herne's Acre.

"But Hen was sick for a short time before she died," he said, "and I don't know if you remember me making a joke about the house being haunted? Right, well, that nonsense started when Hen was, ahhh, indisposed. No-one *really* believed it was haunted, that wouldn't be possible, not here. But—"

"Why not here?" I was surprised.

"Well, because—" he sounded startled. "Well, I mean, I

suppose you hear stories… anyway," he hurried on, "what-ever people believed, things were certainly seen. And heard. Lights and noise and so on."

"Why on earth—someone assuming Hen Rosse was on her deathbed, and wanting the house to look haunted to discourage buyers?"

Dermot shrugged. "That's what we thought."

"If someone had had their eye on Herne's Acre, they might have asked Millar to help them make it look haunted, unattractive to a buyer?"

"If you wanted something dodgy like that, Millar'd be the boy to ask."

"Ivo Collier never had an interest here?" I asked and Dermot laughed. Even Herne's Acre wasn't high-end enough for Ivo, it seemed.

"I heard Ivo had a spat with Millar over prices," I said, "but he rushed off very quickly from Delia's party. He didn't have another row, did he?"

Dermot squashed up his lips, thinking. "I didn't see himself and Millar talking much at all," he said eventually, "Lorcan only invited Ivo for mischief, to annoy Millar."

"Did you happen to see who Ivo *was* talking to before he left?"

Dermot shook his head. "Whoever it was, was in fancy dress, one of the witches. They went off pretty sharpish, too. Then Ivo left."

Dermot left then, and I made the tea I had offered him, cudgelling my brains to recall what I had and hadn't seen on the night of the party. It seemed wrong that someone— especially someone who volunteered so much of their free time to the world of fictional detection—had seen nothing of use when there was a real murder.

Or had I? Fancy dress, Dermot had said. About ten minutes before Ivo hurried away, one of the witches had scuttled through the rain to her silver Dacia with a waterproof prosaically over her head. Might that have been Ivo's correspondent?

Twelve

Herne's Acre and environs, Wednesday 26th October.

IT WAS BEGINNING to get dark, and Pupsqueak had been inside for most of the day, so I fetched the leash for him, and a hi-vis jacket for myself. We walked almost as far as the village, turning back just where the road down the hill swooped to the left, as I wanted to get home before night really set in.

We were approaching the twisted crossroads at the Chapelraymond bridge. One road made its serpentine way around the boundary of Herne's Acre to Heathcote, another road branched north to Pettimills, and the third headed east through thick trees to Cotter's Hill. The little bridge held everything together.

As soon as we stepped onto the junction, Pupsqueak gave a loud, short howl and I jumped like a goosed fox. The dog turned back and pulled on the leash, straining till he almost pulled me off my feet. I was suddenly conscious of a thick, creamy current of shatteringly cold air, so profound and unexpected that the breath I gasped in was loud and involuntary. Very dimly, I could hear chiming, six peals of a distant high-pitched bell.

I trotted in Pupsqueak's wake so he would not choke himself, and when we were off the bridge, I looked back, and to my left, to the north. My tongue dried in my mouth. Along the road from Pettimills, a slender horse and a shrouded rider approached, a few shadowy figures beside and behind, six in total. There was a brightness from them, it was hard to explain the source of the light, and it was so spectral a brightness that it served only to show the horse to be a bay, the rider dark-clothed, with long dark hair.

The only other things visible were hands as pale as pearl, moving— and without even time passing, the horse and its attendants were walking where they would have run me down had Pupsqueak not dragged me away— in the same instant, as though seconds were piling on top of each other, the horse was stepping unhurriedly across the bridge, the rider was combing its long, long hair with a bone-pale comb, there was nothing to be seen of the walking attendants except their shadows, in the same instant that the horse reached the south edge of the little stone bridge, the head of the rider turned.

Pupsqueak leaped, and knocked me off my feet. I crashed into the ditch, and again Pupsqueak silently pounced, keeping me from turning back, from looking back, herding me at the edge of the road where shadows were growing like grass. There was no shred of sound to give me a hint of what was happening.

Finally, Pupsqueak seemed to relax. He trotted away a few steps, licking his snout. I could see the rear of the shadowy and silent passage. The temperature rose, the trees started their gentle rustle as the wind lifted. I raised my head. I tottered to the bridge and, having to brace myself to do it, looked down the road into the trees towards Cotter's Hill. Naturally, it was empty.

Pupsqueak waited in silence beside me. I turned and goggled at him for an explanation, but said nothing for nearly a minute, because I seemed to have forgotten all my words. I started to shake.

But the fun wasn't over yet. Whatever it was that had passed me by was still visible, in a flickering, shimmering sort of way, along the road, with the boundary of Herne's Acre to its left. If such things had a left or a right. The shadowy figures reached the point where Herne's Acre met Heathcote, and both boundaries met the road. An intense light bloomed, dazzling and colourless.

There was a sudden flurry of activity in my field. Through the trees, I could glimpse dark-dressed figures dashing out from among the willows by the boundary between Herne's Acre and Heathcote. This was too much.

I set off, shaky-kneed from fright and panting from habitual inactivity. As we rounded the corner by my yard-gate, Pupsqueak racing like a hunter, me pummelling along cursing my abandonment of hiking, someone on a bicycle took off from the front gate, and sped away. Naturally, I had left on the light in my porch, as a rural road on a late October night is as black as the pit. The cyclist was illuminated for only a moment, so I could see no identifier, just a stout figure in some sort of black-ops get-up and their face covered, on a sturdy bicycle in dark metallic red. Pupsqueak might have caught them, but returned when I called him. A motion-sensitive light switched on as we crossed the yard to the field.

Everything was silent, but right at the back of the field, beams of small torches were wobbling over the little stream and past the poison garden. Through small gaps in the high hedge that marked the boundary of the field, I glimpsed more lights, and followed them with my eye till the bicycles crossed the bridge.

My heart was pounding painfully, and I was shaking so hard I could hardly get my keys out of my pocket. I wondered about calling the guards, but Pupsqueak bounded around, giving everything a good sniffing, without reacting to anything.

I felt rather nauseous as I let us in through the back door. Pupsqueak pranced across the kitchen, though whether relieved that everything was quiet again or proud of himself for his performance, I could not tell. I knelt down and gave him a big hug, scrubbling his head and ears, pouring praise on him. He licked my face and rolled over to get his belly rubbed, so I did that, too. I had remembered to buy some dog treats, so I provided one of these, and then turned my attention to some sort of recuperation for my beleaguered nerves.

There was a bottle of brandy, and a very lovely brandy glass, on the island. They most certainly had not been there before I left. Too bewildered to care, I tottered over, and wrestled with the seal on the bottle. I sloshed some of the Courvoisier into the glass, and held it up to Pupsqueak.

"Thanks, pet," I said, and then waved the glass at the house. "Thanks. Just what I needed."

Perhaps I was losing my marbles. I had some justification.

The brandy did its medicinal duty of quelling my nausea and steadying my nerves. I thanked past-me for having made a dinner that lasted over two nights. I was too shaken even to cook rice, so I ate the stew with bread instead. I locked up, and Pupsqueak and I sat upstairs, he eating his treat and then sleeping, me reading some P.G. Wodehouse. I could not quite believe what I had seen, and I could not countenance speaking to anyone until I had recovered.

Later, when I was letting Pupsqueak out for a last piddle, I went out too (though not for the same purpose), and we both walked down towards the back of the field. I could see tracks through the long grass, but it was much too dark and cold to investigate.

I went to bed but couldn't sleep. I got up again, made some tea, and sat for a while on the sofa with the dog, wrapped in an enormous dressing-gown I had found. I sat at first in silence and then with the radio on, with some trad music playing, that the gentle-voiced presenter told me was the *Humours of Mullingar.* Around midnight, when a Norwegian composer I did not know had soothed my jangled nerves, I went to bed.

Thornapple's Narrative. Commission Headquarters. Wednesday 26th October.
I can't lie, I am terribly pleased with us. We are not yet at the root of everything, we still have more stones to turn over, but I think I can say with confidence that we have cracked it.

Sigune's discovery of humans on an unsuspected bridle-path, using it as a way to cross to the sídhe-side, had put us on the right track. But it was Unfortunate Cray who had given us the opportunity. Therein lay the only disadvantage.

Cray was aware that, once into the Season of Shades and especially coming up to Samhain, passages from the sídhe side to the human side were more frequent. We have an alert system, whereby everyone in Corrbofinn gets a notification when we know the Others will be passing through, and the Border Bell chimes at the moment of crossing, one peal per visitor. It's not that they are hostile or dangerous, it is that every world's rules about etiquette, about how to indicate friendliness and respect, differs. The Others, especially the sídhe, are fine and dandy once you remember to *never make eye-contact.* They take it… badly. It's the main reason it has been so easy to keep the true nature of Corrbofinn pretty much secret from the rest of the country. The sídhe would be angry, and it would be a brave—no, foolhardy—Corrbofinnian who crossed the sídhe.

If it had not been for Pupsqueak, JQ's bones might have been ground to powder, and the fact that she did not know the rules would be neither here nor there.

What Cray had done—on its own time, and of its own volition—was to have gone down to Herne's Acre every time there was a notification. It suspected as I did that the crossing would be used for what the humans called "goblin raids," an expensive form of risk-tourism.

I turned to our captive audience. "Can you explain to my colleague here," I indicated Sigune, "what exactly a *goblin-raid* is?"

Mortals can be funny about Corrbofinn, about all the border-lands. The borderlands all have some sort of reputation, for being 'mysterious' places. Most people put it down to superstition and folklore. Some half-believe it, but what they really believe is that they deserve a *wow* moment. Some say "there's *something* in it," but they are easy to manage: they visit, but they don't see they are being herded along the *beaten tracks*, and they go home happy, decking themselves and their homes in what they call 'sídhe-core', and what we call 'tat'. But some were more determined to pit themselves against the sídhe-side. Hence goblin-raids. Nincompoops risk their interiors becoming widely-dispersed exteriors, by sneaking across and stealing something: a banshee's comb, a goblin's cap, a lock of a sídhe-beast's mane. They were deter-mined to make the sídhe-side yield some trophy to make up for the hollowness and meaninglessness of their lives, if it was the last thing they did. Which sometimes it was.

"These people decorating their houses," one said disparagingly, "sídhe-core addicts. Just consumers, with no idea of what the sídhe are *really* like."

"I'll tell you what the sídhe are really like," I said. "They're really sick of thieving little trespassers like you giving your egos a sugar-rush."

"Ours is a real risk," the other said. "we don't have the safety-net of your special licences. The sídhe are dangerous. Goblin-raiders like us, we experience danger in a *vital* way."

Sigune stood up. "Let me help you with that."

"Sigune," I warned, "don't. This is not the place to reveal your true face. They will tell us everything they know."

"We won't—"

"You can and you will."

"We have rights!"

Cray, to my astonishment, leaned over them.

"Listen, numpties. I can't tell you how many of you sorry-arsed petty thieves we have had to retrieve from over the border, nor how many pieces most of them were in. Doesn't make no nevermind to me, what I can't stand is the paperwork. But I'll suck it up in a good cause. Now tell my boss here what it wants to know or I'll notify the patrol sídhe-side and throw you back over the border myself."

We got all the information they had; it helped, in its incomplete way. It was usual that the organisers of these raids pretended to be of from the sídhe-side themselves, so these fools had been gormless enough to think that they were being led by a púca called Eithne.

The disadvantage to this night's work was this: Cray's work had been *good*. It had shown initiative, perseverance, wit, a solid grasp of procedure. There was no reason why I could not put its name forward for promotion.

The downside was that I could really use its skills in Licensing. It had earned the 'Unfortunate' nickname early in its working life, but in these recent months, it seemed to have really been making a big—now successful—effort. It was only fair that I give its name to our staffing department.

But that meant I would be without its peculiar but effective way of looking at the world. I also knew who its replacement would be: a toadying little grifter called Hixley. Was I just being selfish?

Thirteen

Jessica Quill's Narrative. Herne's Acre, Thursday 27th October.

REGAN WAS COMING around to see the house today, and I was still so shaken by my experience that I was not at all pre-pared. There was not much improvement I could do, but I tidied up, and I followed the advice of an ex-girlfriend from years ago, who had been an estate agent. Get the house into prime position between tidy ("first impressions last") and lived-in ("no-one likes clinical"). Light some scented incense sticks ("nothing says home like cinnamon"), but only briefly ("you don't want it to smell like you're covering something up").

I was upstairs when I heard wheels crunch on the gravel, and I looked out of my window. Regan had parked her teal Saab in front of the garage, and was mincing her way over the gravel in high heels. To my astonishment, close behind her, Niamh Bracken, swooping in on a bicycle.

"Gravel's a devil on any decent shoe," Niamh was saying to Regan as I let them in, and turning to me to add, "though I don't think you're exactly a Blahnik girl, are you?"

I was not sure of what I was being accused, so I just told her it was an unexpected pleasure.

"Just thought I would have a last look over the house," she said, "before it formally goes on the market."

She gave Regan a huge smile, flicking her glance down over the latter's violet linen suit, pausing for a moment over her velvet boots, and then said,

"I see you too intended to make an, ahhhh, early bid for the place."

Regan looked startled.

"If and when I put Herne's Acre on the market," I said firmly, "it will go through an estate agent. Come on, I'll show you upstairs."

But before I could lead the way, there was a knock on the door.

"Another buyer!" Niamh cried. "We're forming a queue!"

It was Theo Solaita. "Sorry," she said, "a bad time."

"It's okay," I said, "this won't take too long, if you want to wait."

Regan flashed a smile at me, and thanked me for arranging the viewing so quickly. For a fleeting moment, she seemed familiar to me, but then I recalled her photograph from the website. She told me again how she had known Hen Rosse, had attended the courses Hen delivered. Regan was very business-like, and looked over the house quickly but carefully, asking questions about heating bills and damp.

"You said you'd be starting up the kind of work that Hen did?" I asked, when we were in the office. "Do you want to see the work-shed outside?"

"Thanks," she said, and we trooped downstairs. I opened the back door, and waited for them to close their coats and pull up their hoods. I waited outside while Regan looked around. It was a murky day of heavy drizzle and no sign of the sun to get going. Everything, even the light, looked muddy.

"Brave going out there," Niamh said to Regan as we returned to the house, "those are real party shoes, and rain is death on velvet. I made the mistake of wearing a velvet dress to that birthday do, remember?" she added over her shoulder to me. "It was raining cats and dogs. Lucky I only had to dash across the yard to the car."

Then she said,

"You know about it being haunted—Regan, is that the name?"

Regan looked at her, startled. I said irritably,

"Nonsense."

"Oh, I heard all about it," Niamh said, turning right around to face me, "lights going on in the dark hours of the morning. One of the neighbours reported these really weird sounds, like hooting and echoing."

Regan looked alarmed. I was annoyed.

"Yes, I heard all about that too," I snapped. "The official explanation is that those things were just set up, done deliberately by someone who wanted to get the house for a cheap price, deter other buyers."

Niamh was taken aback at my tone. "Official?"

"Yes," I said, and at the time, did not think it reckless to continue, "I know that the guards found some… paperwork that might have been relevant to the case."

I was not displeased to see a flash of alarm cross her face, but she recovered quickly.

"That's a relief," she said. Regan and Theo were both looking supremely uncomfortable.

Both prospective buyers of Herne's Acre left then, crunching across the gravel in their unsuitable shoes and posh wellies, respectively. We heard Regan's engine start, and a few minutes later, I saw Niamh sailing by the window on her bicycle. I made Theo and myself some tea, and she explained that she wanted to let me know she had handed over to the guards the book with the papers in it, and that Butler had assured her that they would follow it up. I wondered if they would be waiting for Niamh when she arrived home.

"What was all that about haunting?" she said,

"Oh, Dermot Thompson told me about it. When the previous owner was unwell, all this nonsense about lights and noises started up. I think Niamh got Millar to help her, and he was suing her for payment."

"Are you really thinking of selling?" she asked, and I nodded.

"There's not what you'd call many jobs over here at the minute," I said. "I have friends in England, I've a brother there, and one in Scotland, so I've no close family here."

"You could rent it," she said, "make a decision later."

I hadn't thought of that. I cast my mind back again over my savings. What about staying in Herne's Acre until after Christmas? Houses did not sell well at this time of year. There were more jobs advertised at the start of a year, too. Could I afford to stay, unemployed, at Herne's Acre for a couple of months? Have my solitary festive season here?

Then a word suddenly came back to me from Uncle Tim's will. *Annuity*. Had I remembered correctly? Was I sure I knew what it meant? If there was even enough to tide me over a few months…

Theo was speaking. "…other thing was, I wondered if you wanted to come down to Whalen's pub tonight, see if we can find out anything from Gemma Broderick."

Whalen's Pub, Pallasalee, Thursday 27th October.
Whalen's was very busy by nine on Thursday evening. We found seats to the left-hand side of the bar, the right-hand

side being taken up by the musicians. I was glad to get a seat somewhere that Pupsqueak could lie down without having his tail stepped on.

There was a bigger crowd than I had expected, given that Whalen's was a little pub in the middle of nowhere, but I was told later that the postmaster would take his VW van around a radius of ten miles and give a lift to any musician in the humour to play. There were two fiddlers, one of whom I recognised from Butler's photograph of Gemma Broderick.

I squeezed my way to the bar and got us some pints. The line of people at the bar moved out of my way almost before I reached them, and I had the strange sensation of someone just in the corner of my eye, that I did not quite see.

I am not an aficionado of traditional music, but even I recognised some of the tunes, so it was after the brisk melody of *Drowsy Maggie* had died away that the musicians paused to wet their whistles, and Gemma Broderick came over to speak to us.

She was the most innately cheerful person I had met since childhood, and she wrung our hands with the enthusiasm of someone meeting life-long heroes. Her dark-brown hair was tousled from all the fiddle-playing, and her perfectly round freckled face was very flushed, making her small eyes look very green. She hitched up her floral maxi dress, revealing platform Doc Martens and tights patterned with sunflowers, and plonked herself down.

There was an empty stool to the side of us, and again I had the odd sensation of just missing a glimpse of someone. Gemma seized her pint of cider, took a long draught, and beamed around at us.

"What can I do for youse?"

"I'm sorry to mention it," I said, "but it's about your ex-beau, Tony Millar."

Gemma's face went blank, and then she scrunched it up. I worried briefly that she was about to cry, but instead she started plucking the air around her head, like she was catching feathers. Then her face became very calm.

"Always works for healing the aura," she said, and I was none the wiser. "My energy centres have been all over the shop since it happened. Poor Tony. I mean he was a wee bastard, but still. I had guessed he'd started nosing around someone else even before I was told, so that story is not as upsetting as it could have been. But *murder*."

"You were only at the party a short time?" Theo asked, and Gemma nodded.

"My friend Bridget asked me to come along, said she had a plus-one invitation and that she wouldn't know anyone else at it. I got there before her, and what do I see except Tony, who only last week started a barney because I was spending too much time with my friends, snuggling up to this other woman."

"Horrible way to find out," I said, and Gemma observed that there *was* no good way.

"And you were gone from the party after how long?" Theo asked.

"I got there at about... twenty to, quarter to six. There was no sign of Bridget, and I didn't wait after I'd seen Tony. You probably heard I had a row with him. I was gone by six for sure. Once I was in my car, the radio came on, and there were the news headlines."

"You didn't come back at all?" I asked, and Gemma shook her head.

"I did not. Why would I? I know I'd suspected, but I was still upset. Anyway, you can't very well cause a scene, flounce out, and then *come back*. Your grand gesture would be a bit… flat."

If she was telling the truth, Gemma was gone far too long to have poisoned Millar before she left.

"What did you do then?"

"I drove home. Well, I stayed parked long enough to text Bridget to say I had left already, and then I drove home. Had dinner, made some hot chocolate, and put a Maeve Binchy audiobook on. Soothing the ruffled feathers."

"The, ah, guards questioned you, I suppose?" Theo asked.

"They did, asked all about Tony, how I met him, all the rest of it," Gemma rubbed her face. "When it came down to it, there was not much I could tell them. I didn't know his family or anything—God," she ended, looking at Theo, "you were family, weren't you?"

"Years ago," Theo said, and added, since Gemma looked appalled. "Don't worry about it. How did you guess he was cheating?"

"The usual," Gemma said, glancing around to see if the musicians were gathering again yet. "He was distracted, he took more phone calls out of earshot, he broke dates."

The way she spoke about it made me feel that I had been very naïve about Louise. I could recall now examples of the same behaviour, but I had never put two and two together and made four. Not until I found one and one making whoopee.

Fourteen

My return home to Kirkaller in September had not been what I had expected. The house was quiet when I went in, the dog was out in the back yard. I went upstairs, not certain if I should expect Louise to be home, as she had been working very odd shifts at the hotel lately. We had had a row before I left, which might have been why she did not know the time of my return. Leaving my suitcase in the hall, I went into the bedroom, thinking I might have a shower after my long journey.

It was a most peculiar sensation. Surreal. I wasn't angry or upset, not at that point. It was more like those disorienting moments of recognition in a dream, where you are sorting out your perceptions. I even looked around, as though I might have walked into someone else's house. I said the first thing that came into my head, which was to alert the horrified blonde to the fact that her bra—hurled aloft during centrifugal undressing—was hanging on the lampshade. I went downstairs, picked up the suitcase, and left the house. Louise came racing down the garden path, coat flapping, hair flying. I confess I waited just a few extra seconds so that she had almost reached Gwen when I took off, leaving her standing in the middle of the road in her bare feet with her pyjamas on backwards.

At least it got a guilty giggle from my siblings when I told them. Not one had held back about not liking Louise. They had been fond of my first girlfriend, they had become accustomed to my being mostly single, though they all had a tendency—even Olive, in Canada—to try and introduce me to likely partners. When I moved in with Louise, after Caleb died and Bethune started reducing its staff numbers, Brendan told me bluntly that it was a mistake, Gerard avoided her, and Olive muttered things about "rebound."

I dragged myself back to the present.

"Your friend Bridget," I said, "is that Bridget Earley?"

"It is," she said, smiling at me. "Do you know her? I work in a mindfulness shop in Dublin, and she came a few times for, like, precious stones and essential oils and stuff. We got chatting. Shared interest, you know."

"Do you know why she was late?"

"No," Gemma told me, "I haven't spoken to her since. Did you meet her there?"

"Briefly," I said slowly. "You've not spoken to her?"

"No," Gemma sounded cheerful, "she's missed my calls and hasn't got back to me. Probably away."

I was aware of a pang of anxiety. Gemma looked at me, and said,

"That worries you. Why?"

"I was the only one who saw her at the party. I think the guards don't believe she exists."

"Of course she exists," Gemma was indignant. "Do they think I'm seeing the Gentry Below?"

"No," I said, "I think they think you saw me, got up as Bridget Earley."

We heard the preparatory scrape of a fiddle, and Gemma hastily downed her pint.

"Gotta go," she said, "fiddle won't play itself. See ya. Listen, don't be worrying about the guards. I'll get hold of Bridget, and tell her to get in touch with them direct."

As soon as Gemma had returned to her musical duties, Theo said to me,

"What do you think? Any chance she's guilty?"

I shook my head. She had not had the opportunity, even if her personality had not made it seem unlikely. When the music started playing, Whalen came over to the table, and sat down with us. Pupsqueak sat up, tail thumping, and Whalen petted him, scratching his chin and chest.

"The guards any closer to finding out what happened to Millar?" he asked.

"Not that I've heard," I said, and Theo also shook her head.

"I heard that Delia Fitzgerald was accusing you at one point," Whalen said to me, smiling, "but I think they wondered about me, too."

"Why would you have a motive?" I asked.

"That was the difficulty for them," he said. "They expected that because I was on the bar, that I would have been in and out a lot. Plenty of opportunity to jab him with a booster ampoule."

"To do what?" I was not sure I had heard him aright.

"Those boosters he took, they're liquid, they come in ampoules that you press into your skin. You'd hardly feel it, but it is absorbed quickly."

I had not even thought about the form of the boosters, but had vaguely assumed they were a pill. Would an ampoule be easier to administer covertly?

"I didn't see you around much," I said, "you were at the bar all the time. Well, you came out with champagne once."

"When did they think *you* had an opportunity?" he asked.

"They didn't say, but they almost openly said they thought I had gone there in disguise, as Bridget Earley. Presumably, they thought that the disguise was so that I could commit murder in that persona."

"Your motive being?"

"Delia knew that someone owed him money, she thought it was me. Did you see Bridget?"

"I didn't know her. From the guards' description, I think she got a couple of drinks."

"Did they ask you anything else about her?"

"Only if I had seen you and her at the same time, which I'm sorry to say I had not."

"Well, it won't matter soon," Theo said, "if Gemma gets Bridget to contact the guards."

"Unless," Whalen said slowly, "the guards are right, and there isn't a person called Bridget Earley."

"What?!" I was dismayed at the possibility that Gemma could not dispel the guards' suspicions of me.

"It's just a thought," Whalen said, "it's the name, you see. Gemma said her friend is from Corrbofinn, but while there's no Earleys around here, I knew I recognised it. It's the name of a *bean-feasa*, a 'wise woman' who was tried as a witch in Limerick in 1860-something."

"There are surely other people—" I started, and simultaneously Whalen said that there was more than one Bridget Earley in the world.

"But," he said, "you must surely know Corrbofinn has a bit of a reputation for, you know—" and he wiggled his fingers over his head, "Woooo-oooo-ooo."

"Well—well, yes, I know," I said, "but—"

I had never given Corrbofinn's reputation a second thought, but I knew of it. It has a constant but vague association with *woo*, with claims of *healing* this and *fairy* that, and *sídhe* the other. Not like Newgrange, or the Hill of Uisneach, places that had a definite and tangible feature; but Corrbofinn was subject at Beltane and Lúnasa to visits from wearers of crystals and beaters of drums. I had heard it called sídhe-core; like *cottage-core* with added fairy-dust. "Bridget Earley" from such a place seemed a bit… stereotypical, now that Whalen mentioned it. Like calling a magical Scot Nessie MacHighlander.

"I suppose," I said, thoughtfully. "Meaning what? Someone creating a persona, someone already planning to off Millar, who cultivates Gemma while pretending to be Bridget Earley?"

"It seemed an elaborate a trick to play on anyone," Theo objected.

"They knew Millar was cheating on Gemma?" I hazarded, "And invited her along in the hope that the resulting row would mean Gemma had a motive?"

"But you said the Fitzgeralds knew no-one of that name," Whalen pointed out.

"Karolina said I was not the only uninvited guest," I said. "But that leaves us with even less chance of identifying who this Bridget Earley is. Though it did occur to me it might be Ivo. Ivo Collier. There was something up between himself and Millar. And he was the right height."

As I spoke, I wondered again about Patricia and Millar. What was it he said was her fault?

"Was he?" Theo said, and I recalled she had met him in Whalen's. "He is the same height as you."

"Like Bridget Earley."

"But you said she wore heels," Theo pointed out, and at once my idea seemed impossibly rococo, especially when

Whalen said,

"He would never get away with it, too many people knew him."

"Who, then?"

Millar suing Niamh, who could not have been in disguise. Patricia Hopkins, furious with him, but there in her own person. Any chance Niamh and Patricia had a connection? None came to mind.

"Do you know why Collier left?" I asked Whalen, but he shook his head.

"I know he left in a bit of a hurry, I had to go out after him when he dropped his wallet on the way. But I don't think Ivo would, you know…"

"Might Millar have been behind why Collier left in a hurry?" I asked, and went on without waiting for an answer, "Theo, do you remember Ivo saying he did not see anyone in outdoor clothes?"

"I do," she said, "I can't say I entirely believed him. He made something of a point of the clothes. I wondered if he had recognised who you meant and didn't want to say so. I mean, it's close enough to Hallowe'en for some people to feel safer in disguise."

I turned fully and looked at her. She glanced to her left, between our seats, and seemed disconcerted.

"Superstition, I mean," she said, and Whalen said,

"Plenty of people in disguises. You weren't able to tell the guards who she was, though?"

I shook my head. "But I think it might be someone called Patricia Hopkins, It's just a guess—"

"Oh, I know Patricia," Whalen said, "she set up that business selling expensive pretty things, herself and a couple of school-friends."

"Koré's World," I said, and with faint mockery, added, "Beautiful things for beautiful you."

"Good line, you have to admit," he said. "I believe it is doing very well. Very popular."

"I don't suppose they have anything as prosaic as an office. Is it all online?"

I was surprised when Whalen assured me that Koré's World did have an office, not far outside Lissascaul. Somehow, an office seemed too mundane an element of something as elegant and refined as the aestheticised existence on offer to the Koré's World audience.

"Patricia Hopkins wouldn't hurt anyone," Whalen said. "She has a hot temper on her, but she's never going to do anything as cold as come to a party armed with poison. She doesn't plan that far ahead."

We sat without speaking for a short time, Theo and I drinking, Whalen petting Pupsqueak. I wondered about a professional connection between Collier and Patricia Hopkins. Might Collier be cold enough to come armed with poison? And had he left hurriedly because he knew Millar would die soon? Then Whalen said he had better get back, just as the musicians stopped for another break.

"Grand dog you have there," he said, and went back to work. Pupsqueak put his chin on my knee and looked at me.

When Caleb died, I could not have considered another dog; even now, I could not think of getting another boxer dog. I had remained resolutely dog-less for the rest of my time in Surrey. I hated leaving the house I had rented for years, I was almost tearful on my last day at my job. But in a way, I had welcomed the move to the North of England. I loved the southern landscape and had done the South Downs Way walk more than once. At the same time, my visits north to see Uncle Tim, especially when he had found some rugged new route for us to explore, had been some of the happiest points of my life. Besides, Northerners disembarking from buses thanked the drivers. I felt at home there. But Louise never thanked anyone, and thought country walks and bagging Munros unsuitable hobbies for a civilised person.

I had begun to consider another dog, but Louise already had one, a tiny, frail, over-bred thing with a foul personality. This furious slipper of a beast meant no room for a proper dog. Pupsqueak's chin felt delicate and warm on my knee. I wondered what the rules were about bringing a dog from Ireland to England. Especially one you had adopted in a dream.

Fifteen

Herne's Acre, Friday 28th October
THE FOLLOWING MORNING was the one I had set aside for being a grown-up. I was going to call Past Designs—before breakfast, even!—to see what was what. I had thought about ringing my boss, but realised that I would rather skin rats with my teeth than speak to him again. In any case, such was his integrity and fair dealing, he would probably just not take my calls. Instead, I rang the human resources section, relieved that my call was taken by Arthur Badger, who was both knowledgeable and effective. He was also fairly blunt, and told me exactly what he thought of senior management in general, and the head of his section in specific.

"You can't say that, Arthur!" I protested, giggling. "They'll sack you, too!"

"The number of minorities I belong to?" he retorted. "They wouldn't dare. Anyway, the boss is out, I've the office to myself. I can let down such hair as I have. Now, I might be wrong, but my guess is that you would prefer never to see the inside of this hellhole again?"

The conclusion of the conversation was not what I had expected. Arthur told me all about my statutory notice, my right to serve counter-notice, the amount of leave I had left, and though I was utterly confused by the end, it seemed, astonishingly, very much in my favour.

"So, I don't have to go back into the office at all?" I said, and Arthur said,

"I'm surprised you're still on the phone, flower. Did you have many personal belongings in the office? I could post them to you? Over there in Ireland?"

I thought for a couple of seconds. A mug, I thought. A cardigan. A photograph of Louise nuzzling her highly-strung slipper.

"Nothing that can't be binned," I said.

"Gaan canny, pet," he said, and hung up.

Of any news I could have heard, Arthur Badger confirming that I never had to cross Past Designs' threshold again was peak satisfaction. I had not quite appreciated how much I hated the place. Not having to see my boss, even not having to see the hideous décor, made me feel fit for any challenge. Even the one that came to my door almost immediately.

I had just hung up when I heard Pupsqueak barking, a note of alarm creeping into his voice. I hurried for the back door, jamming a boot onto one foot as I opened it, and pulling the other one on as I hopped out onto the gravel. Pupsqueak was rushing forward and then retreating to avoid the attempts of two men to catch him. These were not the men who had rushed toward me on the night Pupsqueak followed me into the field. One was tall and quite gangly; he was making ineffectual dashes towards the dog as though he were afraid, but more afraid of being thought afraid. The other was small, apart from his paunch, making much more determined rushes at Pupsqueak, shouting angry instructions at his younger accomplice.

They had their backs to me, and Shorty managed to grab the dog but was unable to hold on when Pupsqueak started thrashing like a landed fish. He let go, just in time for me to land a punch on the side of his head. An unexpected blow on the ear is surprisingly painful, and he staggered off, clutching his head.

"That dog is bought and paid for," he shouted.

"You'll have the paperwork," I said. I hated the way my voice shook. Confrontation always made me sound tearful, even when I was actually angry. I pulled out my phone.

"The man I work for doesn't do paperwork," he said.

"Well, explain that to the guards," I said.

"You stole a dog!"

"You're trespassing," I said, "and the dog was on my property. I took it in to bring it to a shelter."

Pupsqueak gave a peculiar yowl, and was looking indignantly up at me. Distracted, I did not see Shorty suddenly rush towards me. He knocked my phone from my hand, sent me staggering, and grabbed my neck.

When she was seventeen, my baby sister Olive was mugged on O'Connell Street in Dublin. One gurrier grabbed her, and when she tried to hang onto her bag, the other hit her in the face, smashing her glasses and splitting her lip. Further damage was averted by the arrival of myself and both my brothers at speed out of the chippers, when the two miscreants decided that the three of us—we are a tall family, Brendan skimming six-foot-six—were more trouble than the childish contents of Olive's bag warranted. So outraged were we, and my father when he found out, that Olive was urged to take self-defence classes. She is not a great joiner of groups or taker of classes, so for moral support, all four of us had gone.

I regained my balance, bringing my arms to the outside of his and crashing my fists onto his elbows to break his grip. The heel of my hand hard against his throat, and he reeled away. Gangly changed his stance as though to run at me, so I braced myself. He dithered, and Shorty shouted,

"Leave it. Leave it, Paudge. We're not paid enough for this."

He leaned his hands on his knees, wheezing. When he had his breath back enough, he straightened up.

"You go ask your friend Molly Thompson about that pup," he said, "and let her tell you who you're dealing with."

Herne's Acre and Lissascaul, Friday 28th October
Scrapping with random petty criminals before breakfast was not my usual way to start the day, and it gave me a surprisingly good appetite. I gave Pupsqueak his breakfast, and scrambled some eggs for my own, making extra toast to have with butter and marmalade afterwards. Two mugs of tea, and I was as good as new.

After breakfast, I went through my supplies to see what I needed, and wrote a list of what I had to buy. I was going to go to Lissascaul and see if I could find Koré's World's office, and hopefully Patricia Hopkins would be there. First, though, I would go back through my emails and see if my memory had served me well.

The email from Uncle Tim's solicitor was easily found, and I skimmed through it quickly. I had been so upset at Tim's death, and so astonished at his change of heart regarding his home in East Linzfield, that I had focused entirely on the question of Herne's Acre. I must have been told at the time that he had bought an annuity for me, but the question of suddenly owning a house in a country I didn't live in had diverted all my attention. Even if I had been focused enough to ask how much the annuity would yield, I knew that they fluctuated depending on interest rates, and I was also sure that it would have been enormously expensive to buy an annuity that would yield an annual income that could cope with rising mortgage rates and increased cost of living. But might it be enough to tide me over a couple of months? I was at least right about the fact of the annuity. I would have to investigate further before I knew how much I could count on. But even that fact, even knowing that I was not under immediate pressure to get a job or find a new home, was enough to lift my spirits.

"Come on, Pupster," I said, and Pupsqueak gave me that unmistakeable look of affronted dignity that clearly demanded *who do you think you are calling Pupster?* But he climbed into Gwen's back seat without argument, and we drove to Lissascaul. I went to the supermarket and while I was paying, I asked the cashier for directions to Koré's World. It took him a moment to place it, but then he directed me out of the town, and to keep an eye out on the left-hand side.

The office was very small, like a small converted cottage, with a flagstone yard in which was parked a two-year old silver Dacia. I had to ring a doorbell, and when I said my name, the response was not exactly welcoming.

"Oh Lord," the voice sighed, "I should have known. I suppose you had better come in."

Patricia Hopkins, when I met her, was neither as casual as I had seen her at the party, nor as glamourous as on her website. She wore a dark suit of some heavy material, and had her hair French-plaited. She waved me impatiently to a seat, and sat down herself, saying as she typed,

"Excuse me one minute, I just need to finish…"

I looked around her office idly while she worked. It was very bright and comfortable. Everywhere were samples of

Koré's World stock: cosmetics, jewellery, phone covers, wraps, hats, oil-burners shaped like owls and cats. Some items had lovely colours, but none of it appealed to me. Too many of them looked like a decoration in search of a function, and all of them were firmly on the twee end of whimsical.

Then she turned, leaned her arms on the desk, and looked at me sternly.

"Ivo told me that you were asking about me. Because of the party."

"I know it probably just seems like rank curiosity," I said, and she pounced,

"Isn't it?"

"Well—yes, in a way," I admitted, and she laughed. "But not only. Delia Fitzgerald accused me of murder, so I had a vested interest in finding out the truth."

"I heard what Millar did to Delia," she said, sombre again. "Little tick."

"You were supplying him with these boosters, though?"

She rubbed her hands almost savagely over her hair.

"Look," she said, "a couple of us set up Koré's World, and we might be friends but we have to pull our weight. Regan's in charge, and she'd throw a baby on the tit to the wolves if she had to."

I tried to keep a straight face, and failed miserably.

"Don't get me wrong, Regan's great," Patricia said, smiling at my mirth, "but she pulls no punches if she wants you to pull up your socks. I was the one who suggested those phone-covers, for example."

She picked one up and waved it at me. It looked familiar, but probably because I had seen one too many 1990s soft-rock album covers in moody black and white, with a vaguely ethereal vibe.

"They didn't work out, only a handful of them sold. Regan was *not* pleased. But I had developed this new work stream, it's a real new departure. I'd really taken ownership of it, it's focused on blending Koré's World creativity with what is sometimes called sídhe-core but that we like to think of as fae-inspired."

She was beginning to sound like an advertisement.

"Is this antiques and stuff?" I said, and Patricia flashed me a reproving glance.

"Soft furnishings?" I suggested, unreproved.

"It is an aesthetic vision," Patricia corrected me. "Koré's World now transforms and elevates homes from mere living areas to truly inspired and creative liminal spaces between the Koré-enriched life and that touch of magic inspired by the sídhe."

I was none the wiser at the end of her sentence than I had been at the beginning, but it wasn't the soft furnishings —sorry, the aesthetic vision—that interested me, nor the hair-splitting of *fae-inspired* over *sídhe-core* since none of it explained her threats to Millar. I pressed her further.

"You've moved to Corrbofinn," she said abruptly, "I mean, you're living here now, aren't you? At Herne's Acre?"

"I'm here for the moment," I said, "but intending to sell."

She blinked a few times, and raised one eyebrow.

"Damn," she said, "that's bad news."

"Why?"

She did not answer, but returned to the question of fae aesthetics.

"Sometimes—you know how it is, you're selling something, you maybe describe it in—more emphatic terms—than is literally true. Caveat emptor and all that. You expect people to understand."

She rubbed her hands over her face.

"Millar bought some—objects from me. A couple of mirrors, a rug, some—decorative objects. But he then sold them on, but he sold them to—someone whose—expectations were different."

"Ivo Collier," I said immediately, and she nodded, looking haggard. I was bemused. What did she mean by *emphatic terms*? Collier was buying this sídhe-core tat, what 'different expectations' could he have had? I did not quite think that Patricia was lying, but I could not put my finger on the way in which she was not telling me the truth.

"And what—"

"I can't go into detail," she said, firmly. "Suffice it to say that—well, I'm facing repercussions. And if Millar had blabbed his mouth off, that whole enterprise would have gone belly-up."

"And you threatened to cut his throat."

Sixteen

PATRICIA FLINCHED. "I didn't kill the little bastard," she said, and she sounded exhausted. "To be honest, if you'd found him with his head stoved in by a hammer, I might have been in the running. But to poison him—that's too cold-blooded for me. Him being dead does me no good. I'm still left with the mess."

"I'm sorry," I said, with real sympathy. "Am I right in thinking that you came back to the party, though? To say something to Ivo?"

"Ivo—bought from Millar in good faith," she mumbled. "I'd only just found out that Millar sold the stuff on, so I was slow on the uptake about the—consequences. I had to tell Ivo."

"You came back to the party? As a witch?"

She laughed.

"Regan says never miss a chance to advertise," she said. "I left Cotter's Lodge to go to another party, I'd planned to wear one of our own witch outfits. I was changing in the car when I realised—well, the consequences, I went rushing back to tell Ivo, and left again straightaway. Here, speaking of advertising—" she held out one of the phone-covers, grinning at me. I laughed, and slipped it over my phone.

"I won't take up more of your time," I said, starting to get up. "Thanks very much for all your help."

Patricia sighed heavily, and shook her head at her screen. I moved to the door as her phone rang.

"Can I ask one last thing? Ivo was seen hanging around Delia's cottage. Any idea why?"

"Probably hoping to persuade Lorcan to renovate. That cottage… has features of interest. Hello? Yes?"

She waved at me, and as I left she said, "Yes, Tricia Hopkins speaking."

Feeling that I had already had an achieved morning, I wondered if I could get a cup of coffee while I decided on my course of action. Cafés did not tend to accept dogs, and indeed, Briody's Café had a sign to that effect on their door. Beside the café was a small bakery, so I tied Pupsqueak's lead to the post of the railing and went inside. I bought some bread, a piece of quiche, and an apple-tart. I drove home, and while I had some tea and a piece of the apple tart, I contemplated my next move.

I had already begun to suspect what was up with Molly Thompson. I had seen the burned-out structures in Millar's back garden, and it gradually dawned on me what they were. The thug who turned up trying to lay hold of Pupsqueak had virtually confirmed it. I was going to go straightaway to confirm. First, I rang Theo Solaita.

"Remember the odd burned buildings we saw behind Millar's house?" I asked, when she answered, "Want to come with me to see if I've guessed right what they are?"

Rather than my picking her up, Theo told me to wait and she would drive to Herne's Acre and follow me to Molly's house.

I knew there was a reasonable chance that Molly Thompson would not be home, but I did not care much. Theo followed me, and I tried to remember that she was not used to the local roads, so I drove slowly, especially over the rough bits, where you could have lost a sheep into the potholes. When we got to Molly's house, I drove up into the yard with a flourish, and as Theo got out, I led the way around the back of the house, tense and angry, and also anxious about what we would find.

The righteous wind was taken a little from my sails at what we *did* find. Six kennels of almost luxurious design. Well-built, cosy, with baskets, blankets, toys. In each one was a dog of a different breed—boxer, cocker spaniel, papillon, Labrador, Jack Russell, and a springer spaniel. Four of them had newborn puppies, the other two dogs were pregnant. Kneeling outside the springer spaniel's kennel was a bald man with a luxurious beard and a jacket that said GOLDEN VETERINARY SURGERY across the back. Hearing us crunching across the gravel, he sat back on his heels, and then, when he did not recognise us, stood up, hands on hips.

"One of the buyers, were you?" he said.

"There's no need to be antagonistic," I said, "we came to see what happened to the dogs."

"Did we?" Theo said.

"Well, they are all fine," he said, "though poor Vita had a rough time of it. But she'll be okay now, won't you, Vita?"

The pregnant springer banged her docked tail against the basket.

"When were you first called out?" I asked. The vet looked faintly surprised.

"Sunday," he said. The day after Millar was killed.

"Were these Tony's dogs?" Theo demanded. "Are these stolen?"

"Twice over," I told her.

We heard the footsteps simultaneously, crunching across the gravel, and we both turned around. Molly was doing a Jackie Kennedy impersonation today: boxy suit, kitten heels, dark glasses, dark brown wig.

"For the love of God," she said, "you had better come in. Is everything okay, Conor?"

"I've just Logan to check, then we're done," the vet said as we trooped away.

"I knew you were a busybody the minute I met you," Molly said to me, leading us into the kitchen. She whipped off her glasses and tossed them onto the table.

"Have you met Theo?" I asked, "Millar's ex-wife? Theo Solaita?"

"How'd ye do?" Molly said. The annoyance on her face, the irritability with which she thrust forward her hand, were at odds with her polite words.

"I suppose you may as well have a cup of tea," Molly said, turning the tap on full so that the water fountained out of the kettle and splashed her suit. "Make yourself useful, and get some biscuits from that press there."

I did as I was told, and Molly switched on the kettle.

"What is going on?" Theo asked, a little plaintively.

"Tony Millar had a puppy-mill," I said, looking at Molly to make sure I was correct. "He kept bitches in those tiny, cramped little kennels at his house, and he kept them churning out puppies—"

"Alright," Molly said, turning away, and busying herself getting cups and saucers. Theo looked at me, horrified.

"Those dogs I saw—"

"Yes," I said, hardly able to bear the thought that some other Caleb had been enmeshed in Millar's horrible industry.

"I thought it was legit!" Molly cried, "I didn't know! I'd been helping to sell the pups, and a buyer got in touch, but wanted to see the pups with the mother. I called Millar to arrange a visit, but he refused. I got suspicious."

"You went up to his house," I said, "and you saw that he had the dogs in those tiny cages, no proper shelter—"

"I know! I know," she repeated, "I know. I couldn't take the dogs immediately, I had nowhere to house them."

"Where did Millar get the dogs?" I asked.

"He just said he had a contact."

"What was their name?" Theo asked, very business-like.

"Reynolds," Molly said, "Bernie Reynolds."

"Twice stolen, you said," Theo said to me, "Reynolds stole good quality dogs, popular breeds—"

"I went back up the night of the party," Molly interrupted, "two days later. I knew Millar'd be away on Delia's birthday. I offered to be Dermot's driver, so he could have a couple of drinks. It meant I could borrow his jeep. It took three runs to get the dogs back."

"How did you get kennels ready so quickly?"

"I—"

Theo, to my surprise, interrupted. "I expect she knows some people, don't you, Molly? People who, *unlike Jessica*, live here."

"Oh— eh, yeah, that's right," Molly said. "You're *leaving?*"

"You stole the dogs," I said, "to rescue them. And then you burned down the kennels."

"I'm only sorry Millar wasn't inside them."

"Good job he wasn't murdered by fire," Theo said mildly. Molly looked too stunned to speak, but then blurted a reply.

"I didn't kill him! Where would I get atropine? I wasn't at the party! You'd have seen me," she added to me.

"I didn't know you," I objected, "and you are a great woman for the different disguises. You could have been there, I wouldn't have known. Millar had your number on a phone with only six contacts."

"I wasn't at that party," she said firmly, "I was stealing half a dozen dogs, terrified one of them'd go into labour on the way, or someone might think I had anything to do with— murder's one thing, but puppy-farming!"

"That's why you wanted the herbs," I said, ticking off that question, "peppermint, fennel seeds, those are all for nausea. You wanted them for the dogs."

We sat in silence for a moment. I had been so angry at realising what Millar had been up to that I felt quite wiped out. Molly was no longer angry, or at least not at me, but while she seemed relieved, she was still anxious. Theo just seemed shocked.

"There's something else," I said to Molly, "isn't there? You're still worried."

Molly blew her lips out, and rubbed her hands over her face. The action knocked off the pill-box hat, and the wig, and once the wig was gone, she took out her contact lenses, too, leaving her black-haired and blue-eyed.

"There is something else. There's this... not friend, business contact, I suppose, of Millar's. He's... I don't know him, but I know of him. He... Millar was kind of afraid of him."

"Oooh," said Theo, "an actual thug, then."

Molly nodded, now looking miserable.

"He wanted to get dogs," she said, "but—like, people buying from him are not just, you know, ordinary Joe Schmoes not paying enough attention to where the pups come from.

They're, you know, rich and maybe no-one asks too many questions."

"Who do you mean?" I asked. "Give us a name."

"Well," she said, uncomfortably, "say someone like Malachi Stone."

"Oh, Lord," I said. "Really?"

Malachi Stone, former television personality, former celebrity sports manager, active entrepreneur, owner of doped racehorses, fixed matches, hastily-developed properties, and shady businesses. A thug in the worst-cut suits money could buy, surrounded by security, sycophants, and every other conceivable form of conspicuous consumption.

"Yes, really. I swear he must spend his days thinking up of rare things he can try and own," Molly said.

"What has he decided he wants now?"

"A dog," Molly said to Theo. "In particular, that dog."

She pointed at Pupsqueak, who put his ears back and lay down, looking uneasily from Molly to me.

"Why?"

"I can't explain."

We lapsed into another silence, broken by the vet knocking on the door. Theo and I had some more tea while Molly went to talk to the vet, but we reached no conclusions before Molly returned. Theo and I took our leave.

"That's the BR initials on Millar's phone explained," I said

"You are getting places," she said. "Listen, why don't we go for a drink in Whalen's tonight? I want to know how you're getting on with the murder. And there is someone I think you should meet."

I accepted, despite the fact that her last phrase was exactly the kind of thing my siblings said when they were trying to set me up with someone.

Seventeen

Whalen's Pub, Pallasalee, Friday 28th October

THEO WAS ALREADY in Whalen's when I got there that evening, sitting up at the bar in a round-backed chair, chatting to the most extraordinarily beautiful person I had ever seen. Theo's companion was about my height, trim and athletic, and the hands that held the glass between them were as shapely as a statue's. Their face was long and wide, the features surely fitting some golden ratio, with elegant bones and the grave serenity of a Byzantine ikon. They had a neat ridge of fur from the back of their head down past the collar of their dark jacket. Their eyes were as orange as an owl's and as bright as Venus. I nearly gave them a round of applause just for existing. So stunning were they that for quite a long time I did not notice that their skin, which gave off a sort of pale violet bioluminescence, was not a single colour, but like harlequin marble in indigo and emerald.

"Jessica," Theo said, "meet Thornapple."

"A pleasure to meet you, Jessica Quill," Thornapple said, holding out one hand. Their skin was marmoreal, too, and weirdly charged. My hand tingled as it was returned to me.

"We have been discussing the murder," they said. Their voice was high and hoarse, but resonant, giving no hint as to likely pronouns. Whalen came out from the back kitchen, carrying a steaming wire basket of shot glasses. He started unpacking it.

"We have a murder on our hands," Thornapple sounded

worried, but faintly excited. "We haven't had one of those in— a while."

I was startled to find Millar's was not the first.

"Do they know how he took the atropine?" Whalen lined up the last of the shot glasses on the counter and put the basket aside.

"I heard that Millar was in the habit of taking what they call boosters," said Thornapple.

"I heard that too," Whalen said, expertly tumbling the glasses upwards to their shelf. Such light as there was caught briefly on their gilded rims, so that they looked like stars falling upwards. He caught me watching them.

"Don't have much call for them," he said, "I lent them to Lorcan for his party."

"I never much liked shots," I said, and he laughed and said you might as well be drinking petrol as tequila if you were going to peg it down the hatch like that.

"How do boosters work?" I turned back to Thornapple. "I know they come in little ampoules—"

"—let me show you." Thornapple reached into their breast pocket and held out their hand, rolling on their pale orange palm a glass cylinder full of clear liquid. One end of the cylinder came to a peak.

"How could it be tampered with?" I took the ampoule and held it under the light. Even as I spoke I saw that the tip of the peak was perforated.

"With difficulty, determination, and a slim hypodermic needle."

"How do you take this stuff?" I asked, turning the ampoule over, and Thornapple took it back. They pressed the flat end, and two tiny metal pins emerged, each with a glittering bead of clear liquid.

"Clever," I said doubtfully, and Thornapple returned the ampoule to their pocket.

"Over-engineered, I think. Such a lot of fuss and expense for a bit of vanity."

"A bit of vanity?" I blurted out. "Is that not taking it too lightly? From the little I saw of Millar and Delia, it verged on coercive control."

"In Millar's case, you're right, of course, it was, but for most people, for someone like Ivo Collier, for example, it's —well, they want a bit of extra glamour."

"It's vanity unless you are like Millar and fundamentally a bit of a bastard," Whalen said. "I suppose what you mean, Thornapple, is that if Millar was taking these, then someone could have doctored his ampoule?"

He finished putting away the glasses, and brought the basket away. When he returned, he picked up three pint glasses, and began pouring Guinness.

Thornapple cleared their throat as for an announcement, and we all looked around.

"Did your uncle Tim Fennimore tell you anything at all about the house he left to you, Jessica? About Herne's Acre?"

I shook my head, and continued shaking it as the litany of questions went on.

"About the true nature of Corrbofinn? About the Hostels? About the Commission? Nothing?"

"Not a dickie-bird," I said, bewildered.

Thornapple sighed deeply, and said to Whalen,

"It is my belief that Jessica Quill should know something of the true nature of Corrbofinn. She should know the truth of what Herne's Acre is."

Whalen shrugged agreeably. Theo said,

"I was hoping we could."

"What do you mean by the true nature of Corrbofinn?"
I asked, naturally.

"What do you know of Corrbofinn?" Thornapple asked.
"Oh, you must have heard things," they added, when I hesitated, "no matter how flaky they sounded."

"Well—the usual, I suppose." I felt terribly awkward, and
afraid of insulting the residents. "Well—alright, since you ask,
I suppose I've heard that people believe that if you swim
across the river at Midwinter, that you will cross into the
sídhe. There's some group or another—they go about dancing
on the hills on Beltane morning, that sort of stuff—they keep
trying to get permission to climb—oh, where is? There's
standing stones—"

"Askilbride," Thornapple and Whalen said together, Whalen
muttering it was for their own safety.

"But it's all just 'haunted house' stuff," I said. "Everywhere
has some sort of superstition. Roads being turned so you
don't disturb a wild blackthorn, or if you turn three times
on a crossroad at Hallowe'en you'll see Lucifer. Don't open
your umbrella in the house. I mean…"

"Have you heard the latest conspiracy theory?" Theo
sounded excited.

"No—did someone from Corrbofinn build the pyramids?
Shoot JFK?"

"That the Tuatha Dé Danann are planning a world coup."

I laughed aloud, and said, "No doubt Nuada can borrow
the loan of Shergar for the battle."

Whalen lined up three pints of Guinness.

"On the house. To welcome Jessica to Corrbofinn."

"Did you know," Thornapple said, "that up until 1980-
something, national traffic laws did not apply in Carrickdunn?
Because," they took a mouthful of Guinness, "it was on the

border between the North and South Ridings of Tipperary, and somehow Carrickdunn fell between, as you might say, two stools. Slipped between the cracks, like a penny through the floorboards."

"I didn't know that, no. From what I've seen of parking in Lissascaul, it mightn't be the only one. What's this to do with—"

"Corrbofinn: the same. It's between two worlds."

I waited, either for them to explain what they were talking about, or for sense to emerge. I waited a full minute, which sounds quick, but sixty seconds, counted slowly, is a meaningful pause. Nothing was forthcoming. Whalen, Theo, and Thornapple continued looking at me hopefully. From the passageway behind Whalen, there was a slightly hysterical electronic beeping, and Whalen left, emerging swiftly with another steaming basket of clean glasses.

"What do you mean by two worlds?"

Whalen looked positively excited at my question, starting to decant the glasses.

"Corrbofinn is an area of about four or five miles squared," he said. "All around it, the regular world. Laws of physics. Laws of chemistry. You die, you're dead. Time does not go backwards. That which is disordered does not become ordered—scrambled eggs don't unscramble, a mixture of ink and water does not separate."

He leaned on the counter, and said,

"Corrbofinn is one of the places where worlds… overlap. Our laws are not the same."

Thornapple added,

"Nothing is familiar anymore once you cross the boundary into Corrbofinn. Plants, animals. The weather, even. Metals, stones. Magic of all sorts. Banshees. Druids. All sorts."

I had nothing to say. What came to mind first—*have you lost your reason?*—seemed rude.

"When you came here first," Theo said, "did anything strange happen? You would have driven in through Shanbaltin. Anything unexpected? Sat-nav lost its mind? Paper map had bits missing?"

I blinked very rapidly at her.

"Well, yes, actually, in fact, yes," I said, "I had to stop and ask for directions. The person I spoke to said it was a sat-nav black spot."

"They would, wouldn't they?" Whalen said. "You're not from around here. What happened was that you came off *the beaten track*, the roads we get the outsiders to stick to. Keep them from seeing things they shouldn't."

There was silence until we had finished our pints. They were clearly waiting for me to believe them. I was so preoccupied that I paid no heed to the silent exchange between Thornapple and Whalen. He finished with the glasses, and started pulling the pints.

"I don't think we've convinced her," Thornapple said, "have we, Jessica?"

I was lost for words. All I could think of was *what are they up to?* That they were spinning me a yarn seemed obvious; what I could not understand was why.

"But I've been to Corrbofinn before," I protested, clutching at some facts, "we used to visit an aunt who had a farm in Terryboltin. We'd go on trips."

"Your aunt Nell," Thornapple said, "will have stuck to the *beaten tracks* if she brought you through Corrbofinn, but I expect you mostly went to Lough Garragh, around there."

"We're not lying to you," Whalen assured me. He laughed

then, and scribbled a circle in the air with his finger to indicate my face.

"Not convinced," he said. "Maybe this will help."

He put his hands flat on the counter, and leaned over so our noses almost touched. I pulled back. He stretched his neck, and heaved a little, like he was bringing up something. The middle of his face bulged out, eyes moving back and becoming big, skin sprouting coarse hair. Before I could see what he would become I was on my feet, the pints went flying, I was scrambling back so fast I got tangled up in my stool and went tumbling, spinning over the floor. I regained my feet, shaken and furious, picking up the stool and striding back to the counter with it in my hand like a weapon. Whalen looked exactly as normal.

"You'll believe us now," he said. "You're not as far from us as you think."

"What do you mean?" I slammed the stool down.

"You're still here. Anyone else would have been out that door like a bullet from a gun, running for home."

"Sorry," he added, and it sounded genuine, "I know it is kind of horrible the first time you see it. But we could talk about it for seven days and seven nights, and we'd never convince you like you are convinced now."

I turned to Theo.

"You *knew*?"

She made a face of apology.

"I work for the same Commission as Thornapple. I'm one of their translators, but I'm based on the borderland in Northumbria."

"And we both worked," Thornapple said, "with Tim Fennimore. He was one of our best diplomats."

I sat down so hard it hurt. Whalen snapped his fingers a

couple of times. The broken glasses vanished, and I could hear shattered remnants tinkling in the bin behind the bar. The spilled drink disappeared too. Whalen started pouring replacements. We said nothing until the head had settled, and Whalen topped them up. Then he set my drink in front of me and said,

"On us."

I looked at the dark and creamy Guinness. To accept this drink seemed a weighty thing to do. It was implicitly saying that I forgave him for scaring me half to death. Maybe even that I believed what I had seen, what I had been told. Then I thought, dammit, Louise turned my life upside down, and she didn't even buy me a pint to apologise. I picked up the glass, and we drank.

Eighteen

Thornapple's Narrative.

JQ HAD THE PUP with her, and I could see why Sigune had gone to such trouble over it. Pupsqueak was a charmer, intelligent, friendly, and well-mannered. I did not mention to JQ about the Wild Hunt rejects. Mostly to avoid hurting the animal's feelings. It is bad enough she named it Pupsqueak.

I can't describe the relief of knowing that at least the owner of Herne's Acre knows its nature. We did not go into all the details, but Whalen was right. Most people would have fled. JQ fell out of her chair, but she didn't run. I did not think it the best time to test out whether she can be persuaded to stay and be our Hosteller, our replacement for Hen Rosse. That can come later. So can explaining her own, her family's connection with Corrbofinn. But I knew from my contacts in Northumbria that her job had been taken from her, and I had managed to use those same contacts to make her departure more advantageous to her than her employer was expecting. If she can be encouraged to think of Herne's Acre as home, she might be more open to the idea of a job with us. Maybe Sigune had been right. The house, the dog, some money—all ties to Corrbofinn. I might take up Sigune's suggestion of having a word with Birhanu to let JQ continue with her investigation. Butler would be intractable, but Birhanu might give JQ a bit of leeway if it would help us have a Hosteller in place. JQ might even help.

I did tell her about the bridle-path, though. She told us of seeing the Others on the bridge, and we explained why Pupsqueak had knocked her down to stop her making accidental eye-contact. Theo explained that the sídhe, though implacable, are not violent, but the difference in our material natures, on one side of the border or the other, can have unfortunate consequences for both (as some sídhe are infinitely tiny on the human side, which is a shock to them), but mostly for the humans. JQ moved the topic on, though, by telling us what she had seen in Herne's Acre after the Others had passed by. I thought it only fair to explain the old tracks, and that what was snuggling the boundary between Herne's Acre and Heathcote was a bridle path.

There are plenty of what we call old tracks, that go from one world to another, or more usually from one time to another. What is running between Herne's Acre and Heath-cote is more rare. It is a small road that evolved through use—a road built by walking, you might say—that joins one of the five great roads from the Hill of Tara and that also leads to the sídhe itself. Much more unusual, and often no longer complete. That was where she found Pupsqueak. I told her about those who pursue their sad thrills through goblin-raids and she promised to keep an eye out for activity.

She took it all well, really. Considering.

Jessica Quill's Narrative.

An unusual feature of Whalen's is that it serves a low-alcohol draught beer called Monster Beer, that really is very good. So, though I stayed late in the pub, I was sober when I got home. The whole evening had been so peculiar that I did not want just to go straight in and do something mundane like make tea. When Pupsqueak ran out into the field, I followed. We walked the whole way around the field, ending on the side where Thornapple said the bridle path was, but everything looked very ordinary in the night. I walked down to where I had seen the figures scattering at a run the night the Others passed by. All signs of activity had gone. We continued our walk, Pupsqueak and I, stopping again at the poison garden gate. I looked back up towards the house, and inhaled deeply, smelling dug earth, the cold damp air, and mandrake.

A walk on a windy night, under the star-flecked cloud, wound down the odd evening, and my sense of being too stimulated for the ordinary began to fade. I realised I was cold, and Pupsqueak and I made short work of the walk back to the house. I gave the dog a drink, and I made some tea for myself, along with a little toast to soak up whatever alcohol was in my system. Then Pupsqueak and I sat on the sofa listening to a radio drama, but because we had arrived in the middle, I never found out its name.

Before I fell asleep, I thought back to the appearance of the Others on the bridge, and I hugged Pupsqueak closer. I thought back to the figures scattering, those I knew now were on this 'goblin raid' Thornapple described. And I remembered something. A figure in black, cycling away at top speed on a bicycle that I had seen, metallic and red, in the brief flash of the porch-light. And Niamh Bracken, cycling away at normal speed after her unannounced visit to Herne's Acre, also on a bicycle. A metallic red bicycle, to be exact. Perhaps I should go and talk to her about it.

I did not have time to go to Niamh's house until early evening the next day. I spent the day getting in touch with the solicitor, and finding out the implications of the annuity that was part of my inheritance. The solicitor sounded impatient with me for not having found out the details before now. I simply had never thought that, with all the expenses I had, I could conceivably inherit enough money to make a difference to my need for paid employment. Ending the call, I realised how inattentive I had been to my good luck.

Then I contacted Brendan, to explain that I would stay in Herne's Acre until after Christmas, when I expected both the house and the job markets to be more vibrant than in the dying months of the year. He sounded a bit doubtful, and asked the usual big-brother questions about being sure I had considered all my options. But Brendan knows me best of my siblings, so he had no difficulty understanding that a Christmas alone was not an admission of failure or defeat, but an embrace of a love of one's own company.

Niamh Bracken's House, Pettimills Road, Saturday 29th October

It took only a few moments in Gwen to get to Niamh's house. The roads were empty, apart from a cyclist braving the day's peculiarly thin but drenching rain, passing me at the bridge, and a van I recognised as the local electrician's, heading home. Niamh had a renovated cottage, set a little back off the road, with a lawn in the front. I pulled into her driveway just as the twilight drained into night, and no sooner had I made the turn than I jerked the car to a halt, spraying up a little gravel. Her front door was open, light from the hallway spilling out and making the heavy drizzle glow as it fell.

Niamh was in a suit, the same tight fuchsia-coloured outfit I had seen before. She was lying on the driveway with her legs folded under her, as though she had fallen to her knees, and then slumped over. I thought she was dead, but when I touched her shoulder, she looked up. Her eyes were extremely dilated, and I had the horrible sense of déjà vu, that I was looking again at Millar's dying face, his booster-altered eyes dilated, his mind galloping astray. I could smell something, a very faint scent, sweet and fruity. Niamh's breathing was horribly laboured, but she struggled to get up. *At least she knows someone is here*, I thought, *she knows there's a chance of help.*

"I'm getting an ambulance now, Niamh," I babbled, trying to help her sit up, and get out my phone at the same time, "you'll be fine, you'll be grand."

She slumped against me, but she seemed slightly less advanced towards death than Millar had been.

"What happened?" I babbled on, not expecting an answer, but you never know. "Was there someone here? What did you take?"

Her head lolled, and she made some strange noises that might have seemed to her like words. I grabbed her chin, and sniffed her breath. Wine. Something else, something harsh. Atropine again? Not as sweet. Something earthy. I wondered if I could get an emetic down her throat. The possibility of helping her focused my mind.

"I'm going to lay you down, Niamh," I said. Dialling 999 with one hand, I struggled out of my coat, kneeling on the sharp gravel so Niamh could lean against me, switching the phone from hand to hand. I told the dispatcher what I needed, and the reassurance that an ambulance was on its way was enough to make me feel as though everything was already solved. I put my coat on the ground, and laid Niamh gently down on her side.

"Stay with us," I said, "stay with us. There's an ambulance, paramedics on the way. You've been poisoned, so I'm going to try and get you to vomit. Sorry about it, but to be honest, a bit of sick's not doing that suit any harm. I'm just going to leave you here a minute, to get some—"

As Millar had before her, Niamh suddenly moved, and grabbed my arm. She raised herself up a few inches, and said something to me, so muffled and strange it sounded like a recording played too slowly. *What* I said, *What?* She struggled to speak.

"Don't," I pressed, "don't get worked up. We want the poison out of your system, not your heart pumping it about by the new time. Lie—"

"Hills" she mumbled, "*bridges.*"

"What?" I repeated, feeling a terrible chill of helplessness. Niamh relaxed and lay down. "This is bad enough without you getting weird," I shouted at her, "stay with us, tell me about infrastructure later."

I pulled the edge of my coat over her, and ran to the kitchen. Despite my anxiety and shock, I pulled myself together enough to stand still for a few seconds, smelling the air. I was aware that I looked a bit like a Red Setter trying to pick up a scent, but if there was any chance Niamh had something useful like ipecac, it would be best to know. She did not. I started pulling open all the presses, and the fridge, looking for mustard, running back every few seconds to shout encouragement at Niamh. I found a jar of mustard, and hurried back to the door to shout some useless reassurance. Niamh was up on her elbow, so I rushed to her side. She flopped her head to one side, looked at me, and spoke.

Then she died. I was still holding her, and the jar of mustard, when the ambulance arrived. It started to rain.

Lissascaul Garda Station, Saturday 29th October
"*What* did she say?" Birhanu sounded disbelieving. *Here we go again* I thought, *I drench the chairs while he suspects me of murder.* The garda station was a lot less comfortable than Lorcan's sitting-room, but there were some familiar sights: Birhanu's pen poised, Butler eyeballing me suspiciously.

"She said *fetch*," I said. Niamh's last word had bewildered me, mainly because in my shocked state I was still thinking about setters and scent, and I thought she was giving me an instruction. Butler looked at Birhanu.

"A fetch brings death to a person."

"That sounds like she was saying you killed her," Butler said to me.

"No, it doesn't," I snapped. "If she had thought that, presumably she would have said something clear like *murderer* or *killer*. The fetch is not the cause of death."

"Your fingerprints are—"

"All over her kitchen, yes, I know, I do know how it works," I could not stop sounding angry. "That's because I was looking for something to make an emetic, get her to vomit out at least some of the poison."

"What poison was it this time, do you think?" Birhanu spoke quickly, like he was heading his boss off from antagonising me.

"I think it was mandrake," I said, and realised for the first time that I was still holding the jar of mustard. "I could smell it on her breath. It has much the same effect as atropine."

I was abruptly exhausted. I banged the jar of mustard down on the desk.

"I'm going home now."

Butler said curtly, "We have—"

"I don't care. You're questioning me as a witness, not a suspect. If I'm a suspect, I'm answering no more questions till I get a lawyer."

"I was going to say," Butler said, still sounding tight and curt, "that we have an officer waiting to take you home. We had your car brought to Herne's Acre."

"Oh," I said. "Thank you."

"We will need to speak to you again," Birhanu said, and gave me a tiny, tiny smile. I could not be certain if that meant he did not think I was a double-murderer, or if this was some kind of good-cop, bad-cop deal. Maybe I read too much detective fiction, watched too many shows. We don't even say *cop* here. Though good-garda, bad-garda does not have the same ring to it.

"Grand," I said. "Do what you need to do. I'm not going anywhere."

Nineteen

Herne's Acre, Saturday 29th and Sunday 30th October
WHOEVER HAD BROUGHT my car back to Herne's Acre had
not only parked it in the garage but had brought in my shopping and put the perishables in the fridge. They had even
left a scribbled note reminding me that the clocks went back
tonight, for which I was immensely grateful as it hadn't even
entered my head. I started to wonder how they had managed
about keys, but at that point, everything about Corrbofinn
seemed so weird and overturned that nothing was surprising.
(Thornapple told me later that there are facilities and rules
for such situations, and that the garda in question had
probably been trained by a púca to pick locks.)

I was too exhausted to cook the meal I had planned, but I
had fortunately also bought some pasta and pesto, so I had
the simplest dinner in the world, a belt of the brandy I had
found on the island, and watched *The 4:50 from Paddington*,
the 1987 one with Joan Hickson.

When I got to bed, I lay awake for a while, trying not to
think about Niamh Bracken. *Hills*, she had said, and *bridges*.
Fetch. There was something scrabbling in the undergrowth
of my mind, some reason these words were connected, but
I could not unearth it. I had thought Niamh the likeliest
candidate for Millar's murderer, but presumably her own
death proved her innocent. Or *was* Niamh off the hook?
Had she killed Millar and now someone else had killed her
in revenge?

Once I had fallen asleep, I slept very deeply, and felt refreshed though I awoke relatively early. It had rained heavily during the night, and the morning air felt clear and invigorating when Pupsqueak and I went out.

The sky was clear and pale blue, with a hedge of clouds all around the horizon, grey but thin enough that they looked silky and lambent with the rising sun behind them. Pupsqueak ran all around the yard and I, struck with a random idea, went over to the long shed that had been Hen Rosse's workroom. I had not been inside it since I had been told the extraordinary story of the 'true nature of Corrbofinn', and in retrospect, I think I just wanted to see if anything seemed different in light of the news.

The workroom was clean and bright. There was a wooden table in front of the window, and along the wall that faced into the field, there was a long counter of shining steel, and above it, shelves and glass-fronted cabinets. This was where Hen Rosse had made her tinctures and oils, so beloved by Regan, and Gemma, and Koré's World. Under the counter there were steel shelves holding equipment whose function I could recall from my days in the *materia medica* museums. Some of them looked distinctly antique. I wondered if she kept them for display when teaching her courses. Then I remembered what I had been told about Corrbofinn and realised I still had a great deal to learn. I opened a few drawers, and was struck by how clean everything was, even though it presumably had not been used since Hen Rosse's death. I opened a press above my head, and Pupsqueak came bounding in to see what all the noise was about when something shining and hairy fell out and hit me in the face.

It was a wig. Auburn, curly, bobbed. I looked into the press, and saw that a pair of glasses, with blue metallic frames, were folded and tucked neatly into a space between some glass jars. I crouched down and without touching it, I peered at the wig. Tangled in its curls was a glass cylinder full of clear liquid, formed into a peak at the top. The last time I had seen one of those was in Thornapple's palm when I was being introduced to a booster ampoule.

"I presume," I said to Pupsqueak as we went outside, "that was the ampoule that was supposed to have killed Millar. Because if my sense of smell has not let me down, Niamh was not killed with atropine, but with mandrake."

There was no point worrying about fingerprints, so I shut the bolt on the door. Mandrake. Why had I been thinking of mandrake recently? Not because I was digging it up to kill anyone, but why?

Because I had smelled dug earth and mandrake when I was walking near the poison garden the other night. Someone took the murder weapon from Herne's Acre. Someone was setting me up. I sighed resignedly, and took out my mobile phone.

"I wouldn't be surprised if he arrests me on the spot," I said, and when Birhanu answered the phone, I told him he might want to come around to Herne's Acre and look at what I suspected was the detritus of Bridget Earley.

Herne's Acre, Sunday 30th October
I had just made my first cup of tea when Birhanu arrived, with a couple of cars full of garda officers and Wellington boots. With Pupsqueak keeping a close eye on the guards, I walked with Birhanu down to the back of the field, a cloud of the constabulary in our wake.

"I have not been into the poison garden," I said to Birhanu, "I can't promise there isn't anything dangerous in there. I don't think so, but I can't promise."

"Masks on, lads," said the uniformed sergeant at Birhanu's nod, and all the guards took out masks: not dust-masks, or the sort a doctor might wear, but hideous apotropaic masks with extra eyes, fangs, and with writing along the side. "I, ah, just meant poisonous plants," I muttered. Birhanu said the masks were effective against many things. He gave some brisk orders to the constables, that they were looking for mandrake, and any evidence of who might have been recently in the garden. Birhanu got evidence bags from one of the officers, and put the wig into one and the glasses into the other.

"I suppose you and Butler still think I am the one who invented Bridget Earley," I said. The grass between the crops of trees was long and damp, whipping old rain over our boots.

"I'm afraid so. We have hunted high and low for Gemma's friend, but every lead she could give us was dead-end. At this stage, even she accepts that there never was a real person. She's pretty upset."

Birhanu would not let me go into the poison garden, so I hovered on the edges, looking in. It was very overgrown, and my fingers tingled at the thought of bringing it back to good condition. At least, I hoped that was why they were tingling—who knew what grew in a Corrbofinn poison garden? Laurel and brambles pushed out through the railing, the leaves of the latter dank and spotted, sheltering some decaying berries. The double-gate was fully open, though pushing it over billows of dead grass and against unpruned blackthorn and laurel had given the guards some difficulty.

The first thing I noticed was a large, spreading wormwood plant that seemed to mark the point where the overgrown paths I could just discern converged.

"Here," I said, pulling my attention away from trying to smell what plants awaited me and back to the murder, "I found out something on Friday, I meant to let you know but, well, Niamh…"

"Tell me now," he said.

"Remember I told you that I saw someone with a ponytail threaten Millar? Well, I found out who it was. Her name is Patricia Hopkins."

"Hopkins, Hopkins—Koré's World Hopkins?"

"The very same. And I know why she was threatening him. At least—I know part of the reason. And I might be able to guess the rest."

"We can do our own guessing," Birhanu said firmly, but then cleared his throat, and added more mildly, "Tell me what you know."

"Patricia told me she sold household stuff, what they call fae-inspired aesthetic or something like that, but basically mirrors and rugs and all sorts that are supposedly inspired by the sídhe. Now, Patricia said there were some things that she exaggerated about them."

"Exaggerated what?"

"This is where I am guessing. Between the time I spoke to Patricia and now, Whalen and someone called Thornapple have…. they've explained Corrbofinn to me."

I looked up at Birhanu to see if further explanation was needed.

"You mean…?"

"The true nature, the borderlands, yes, the whole nine yards. Patricia might have been cagey because I *didn't* know then.

My guess now is she sold things as being *actually* made by the sídhe, but they weren't. Though mind you," I thought about my idea, "is that likely? If she said she sold you a magic mirror, you'd notice if it just hung on a wall, not saying nuts about you being the fairest of them all."

"I don't know, though," Birhanu said, "people who are from Corrbofinn, whose families have been here a long time… being so close to the sídhe, to the borderlands, has an effect on a lot of people. Gives them certain… abilities."

"Like being able to hear me shouting outside a house where a party is going on?" I guessed again, and Birhanu smiled. We both turned towards the garden as we heard voices raised, but they died down again. I could see figures in those wild masks, moving up and down the weedy brick paths that radiated out like a sunburst. The morning light was weak, and at this time of the year, nothing was flowering. I saw laurel, yew, the dead sepia stalks and umbels of hogweed. My sense of smell told me that some of the dormant rosettes I could see were foxglove, maybe monkshood. In the still air, the sounds of shovels digging and clay rattling into buckets were very clear.

"Sometimes people can do useful things with the little dab of magic they have," Birhanu said, "sometimes it's just party tricks. I knew a chap in school could turn butter to ice. What good is that? But say Patricia Hopkins could add enough fairy-dust to her furnishings to convince people who have never seen *real* magic?"

"Okay—say she has a lucrative line in selling tin-can Tinkerbells. But the problem was that Millar sold on the ones he bought. Here's another guess, based solely on the fact that Collier left in a hurry. Was it to Collier that Millar sold these things? What if Collier used in a renovation something that was supposed to be made by the sídhe, but was just a normal thing with sparkles?"

"Well—oh, goodness, it could be disastrous!" Birhanu looked very startled. "Depending on whose house he was renovating."

Just as I glimpsed this potentially fascinating line of enquiry, the constabulary began to return. We all trudged back up the field, some of the guards carrying buckets into which they had taken up samples of earth, a couple of casts of footprints, and of plants including—I knew from the smell —mandrake. There was a photographer, too, and as she clumped up ahead of me, she dropped her mask. I picked it up and looked at the writing. It said, *Property of the Garda Síochána. Not to be worn by civilians.*

I was not sure of the etiquette of having your property searched. I hung about awkwardly while the guards packed their buckets and masks into the cars, and Birhanu stood to one side on a phone-call. When he had finished, he said I might as well go inside while he made another call, because he needed to ask me more questions.

Just in case I thought that Corrbofinn had no further surprises for me, I had barely put the kettle on when Birhanu knocked on the door. I waved him in. Behind him were Theo and Thornapple.

"Inspector Butler knows that I am here," Birhanu said, "but not about these two. She's a great stickler for proper procedure. As I am myself," he added, closing the door and following us in. "But she is reluctant to let the… idiosyncrasies of Corrbofinn influence an investigation."

"Whereas you?"

"Whereas I understand that sometimes we need all the help we can get. No tea for me, thanks."

"Coffee? I've only instant, though."

"No, thanks. I don't drink caffeine."

That floored me momentarily. I had literally never met an Irish person who did not drink tea or coffee.

"I have… apple juice? Um… cocoa?"

I saw him waver, and I whipped out the cocoa tin and a saucepan before he could demur. Thornapple, who had been holding their hands behind their back, revealed a bag of croissants and a pot of cream cheese. I am fussy about animal-based food, and go without if I can't afford organic. As though they read my mind, Thornapple said,

"It's from the Others' side. Your best standards are the minimum over there. The animals there have… protection."

I set out the crockery, made tea, boiled up some milk and made cocoa, and when we were all settled with our refreshments, I said to Birhanu,

"Did you find anything worth looking for in the garden?"

"I doubt it. We got some casts of footprints, but I bet you your thief will turn out to have nicked boots from your workshed. Other than that, just enough to show that the mandrake probably was stolen from here. No useful threads snagged on thorns, or conveniently dropped phones or anything."

"Where do we stand, then?"

"I'll start by warning you that we think you have a stronger motive for killing Niamh than you had for killing Millar."

"Because you know about the bridle-path, and the goblin-raids?" I said, noting in passing the peculiar adaptability of the human mind that meant I was using these phrases as though I had not had the wits shocked out of me with them a bare two days ago. "And you think that maybe I knew more about them that I am admitting, and I wanted to be the one in charge of whatever scam it was Millar and Niamh had cooking?"

"That is about the size of it," Birhanu said. "We were round to Niamh's after Theo Solaita brought us those papers she found, and which I am sure you saw. Niamh denied everything, but it was a hopeless hopeless to try to cover her tracks at so late a stage. Between them, Niamh and Millar had worked out a set of quite clever tricks with fireworks and timers and what have you to make Herne's Acre look haunted. Butler's idea is that you wanted to wangle your way in. But on the other hand…"

He took out the little plastic bag in which he had dropped the ampoule. "This makes me think you did not do it, and that someone is attempting to set you up."

"What makes you think that?" I asked, "I mean, I'm delighted, but why?"

"Because it has been widely assumed that Millar was killed when atropine was administered to him using a booster ampoule," Birhanu said, tucking the bag away, "but this morning the coroner told us that the atropine had been administered orally. Meaning someone assumed we would go along with the booster theory, and tried to frame you with the ampoule. Bet you an apple to an acorn it will have been contaminated."

I had not realised how anxious I had been about the possibility of being thought guilty of murder until Birhanu had indicated I might be off the hook.

"Why don't we go over the whole thing," I said, cheerfully, "and see where we stand?"

The coroner's final reports had arrived just as Birhanu was leaving the garda station. The problem, as Birhanu outlined, with poisoning someone at a party was the difficulty of getting anyone to take an individual plate or glass without it looking suspicious.

"Guests helped themselves from a buffet," I said, "and at least one of the catering staff was usually there. When I arrived, Jamie brought me over, but it would have been hard for him, for example, to press a particular portion of food on me."

"Might it have been easier for drink?" Theo said, and then answered herself, "Even at that, I suppose people helped themselves off trays."

"And Whalen was in the bar all the time," I said, "making it hard on anyone to sneak a potion into a glass."

"Didn't Agatha Christie have a story in which a murderer managed to get a person at a party to take a particular glass?" Theo said. "Which one was it, now?"

"*Three-Act Tragedy*."

Thornapple, Birhanu and I had spoken simultaneously, and I added,

"But the killer there had two advantages. He had a small number of people, and an old-fashioned coat."

"Do you think the two murders are connected?" Theo asked Birhanu.

"I hope so," he said. "It seems likely. It could be that Niamh killed Millar, and someone has killed her in response."

"Revenge?" Theo said.

"Or maybe someone else was involved in whatever her beef was with Millar," I said. "I was thinking about this last night."

"Spill," Birhanu said, taking another croissant. "You make grand cocoa, by the way."

"I aim to please. You're very trusting, taking cocoa prepared by someone who might have poisoned two people."

Birhanu looked briefly alarmed, and said, "Nearly worth it for cocoa this good."

Twenty

"Niamh was up in my face over buying this house from the first time I saw it," I said. "Delia's delusion that I killed Millar was based on something she overheard. She knew someone owed money, and she thought Millar said *you're the niece, sell it*. I think what happened was that when Niamh found out she could run goblin-raids, for enormous fees, from Herne's Acre, she determined to get hold of it."

"She was to *get the niece to sell it*," Birhanu said.

"She thought she'd scare me into a lower price," I said, "making it look like Herne's Acre was haunted, saying there would be no other buyers. She gets Millar to help her with this 'haunting'. Naturally, he wants payment. She was counting on paying him from her goblin-raids."

I ate the last of my croissant, and as I wiped my fingers, Birhanu said,

"Millar was suing for payment for the work. Might she have killed him to avoid being sued? Avoid scandal? Seems a bit extreme."

"Maybe not," Thornapple remarked. "She would need an unblemished reputation for genuine otherworld connections if she was hoping to get a foothold in that particular market-place."

"If he had been killed using a booster, she would have had an opportunity," I said thoughtfully, "because she was alone with him in the yard, and she lied about it. But did she have an opportunity if not?"

"Who did have opportunity?" Thornapple asked, refilling our tea-cups. I offered more cocoa to Birhanu, but he refused.

"I thought of Jamie," I said. "He had motive because of the way Millar treated Delia, and because Millar had humiliated Jamie himself that evening. He was moving around a lot during the party, and apart from the caterers and Whalen, he had most opportunity to doctor something and then hand it to Millar, being helpful. Here's your glass of wine, here's your blini. But poison suggests pre-meditation, and why would Jamie have murdered him in so public a way when he had ample opportunity every other day?"

"The same would be true of Delia's parents," Theo pointed out. "Who else is there?"

"Might it have been Collier?" I asked, and Birhanu told Thornapple and Theo our speculation that Collier had been sold fake sídhe-goods by Millar.

"Oh!" Thornapple exclaimed. I later learned that *oh!* was civil-servant-speak for *Jumping Jerusalem, Batman!*

"There was an emergency pass requested on the sídhe-side the night of the murder," Thornapple said. "An antiques dealer called Cecht came over. Now, the address he gave was a house that is being renovated *by* Ivo Collier *for* the new Representative of the Isle of Apples. Might that mean Collier put these supposedly sídhe-goods into the Representative's home?"

"Ivo'd be proper gutted!" Theo exclaimed, then made a face and added, "In more ways than one."

"It certainly would be very serious," Birhanu said, scribbling a note with one hand, and scrubbling Pupsqueak's ears with the other. "I'll talk to Collier this very day."

"There's another thing," I said, rummaging my notebook

out from a pile of stuff on the island and looking down the list of numbers I had taken from Millar's phone.

"BR," I read, "I think that's Bernie Reynolds. Millar was running a puppy-mill, but I don't know of any problem between—"

"Bernie Reynolds," Birhanu said grimly. "We've been trying to get him for months. We knew something was up, we were trying to track down the stolen dogs, but we couldn't get a bead on where they were taken."

"He tried to take Pupsqueak," I said, flubbling the dog's ears. "And—there is someone I know is involved. Unwittingly. She didn't know about the thefts, or about how the pups were being bred."

"I'll need her name," Birhanu said.

"I know," I said, "but I have a feeling she'll contact you herself. She stole the pregnant dogs off Millar and is taking care of them."

"I need her name," he repeated.

"She accounts for the MT on Millar's phone," I said, and when Birhanu protested again, I added, "If she hasn't told you by the end of tomorrow, I'll tell you. Promise. And also, listen, this person—she told me that Reynolds had tried to steal Pupsqueak for—you know Malachi Stone?"

"Oh hell." Obviously Birhanu did know Malachi Stone. "Millar had his number, didn't he? That was the MS. And there was a TH."

"I think that was Patricia Hopkins. When I was at her office, she answered the phone saying *Tricia Hopkins*."

"The MS and the MT numbers were the ones we got no answer from when we rang them. Was anyone else interested in the house?"

"Regan O'Moore, but I don't think she had any connection

with Millar. If she knew about the goblin-raids, and there is no sign that she did, she might have wanted the house. That conceivably gave her a motive for killing Niamh, but not Millar."

"You didn't know this Regan O'Moore before she contacted you?"

I shook my head. "She's Hopkins' boss in Koré's World. Beautiful things for beautiful you," Theo and I spoke the last line together, and Birhanu laughed. I added,

"What Whalen called eco-tat. This sort of thing." I waved the freebie phone-cover Patricia had off-loaded.

"We can move on to Niamh in a moment," he said, casting an unfavourable glance at it. "Can you go through once more who you saw speaking to Millar, who might have been close enough to get a dose of atropine into him?"

I closed my eyes to picture it. Jamie had been near everyone at some point or another. He had almost throttled Millar with a piece of cake, but he had not had time to lace it with poison. Ivo had been talking to Millar just before Ivo left, but if the booster was not the means of poisoning, then Ivo had no opportunity.

The same was true of Niamh, and it seemed to me that I had been in sight of either Niamh or Millar the whole night. Millar had been flirting with Bridget Earley—or whoever that really was—but he was not eating or drinking anything when I saw them, and the problem still arose there that Whalen and the caterers had been overseeing the food and drink all night.

How could any of them have got a strong-tasting poison into him? Coffee was the most likely option, because of its bitterness, but I had not seen Millar drink coffee. *Nothing less than eighty proof passed his lips*, Jamie had said.

"Let's think about Niamh, then," Birhanu said. "I know you told us what you know, but go over it again. See if you remember anything."

I recounted the story. I had gone to see what Niamh would say if I told her I had seen her on Herne's Acre. She had been close to death when I found her. She had said unconnected things about hills and bridges, which I assumed was because she was delirious.

"Where did she live?" Thornapple asked. "She wasn't trying to say something about where someone lived?"

I thought about it, but could not recall any such landmarks. I had seen no-one apart from the cyclist and the electrician. My guess, from the smell of Niamh's breath, was that she had been given mandrake in wine.

"The only thing that I noticed, and I can't remember if I told you, is that she was in business clothes. I wondered if maybe that meant she was meeting someone. Someone coming to the house for some reason."

"We've taken her laptop and her phone," Birhanu said, "and whatever business papers we could find. We might get lucky and find an appointment."

Birhanu left shortly afterwards, and I promised I would let him know if I found out anything else.

"Don't go poking about," he said. "If these murders have anything to do with Herne's Acre, you're already too much involved."

Thornapple turned to me when Birhanu had driven away. "I have promised to show Theo a lovely little café where I often have lunch. Would you like to join us? It's just up the road in Shanbaltin."

"Do," Theo said. "A change of scene might scare up some new ideas."

"Will Pupsqueak be allowed in?"

"Naturally," Thornapple said, but with a slight edge to their voice that suggested I had been a little tasteless in even asking. "There's a farmer's market there, too, if you are interested in that kind of thing."

Theo turned to me. "Did you ever go to the Fenhurst Market when you were visiting your uncle?"

I remembered it well, Uncle Tim had done most of his shopping there. The grocery bill was eyewatering, but the food was delicious.

I half-expected Thornapple and Theo to have some mysterious way of travelling about, something more… Corrbofinn than simply driving along the roads. But Theo had her car, a dashing dark-grey coupé, and Thornapple climbed in while I took Gwen out of the garage.

Shanbaltin, Sunday 30th October
The church where I had stopped to get directions after my sat-nav lost its reason was on the far side of Shanbaltin itself, but the village was in a slight dip so the ruin was still visible, black and blotchy against the rain-grimed sky.

I parked in behind the tiny library. The high street was a long one, broken about halfway by a square that was lined with trees and was currently filled with tents shielding both sellers and buyers from the thin but cutting wind. An outdoor market in Ireland is a brave choice, and I felt sorry for the sellers, standing there for hours guarding their wares. Nine out of ten of them were so bundled up in coats and shawls and scarves that they had the shape and flexibility of small submarines. The remaining one in ten seemed impervious to the cold, scorning all but the smallest neckerchief, and some fingerless gloves.

I had not hoped for much beyond home-made preserves, confectionery and bread, but in fact there were several stalls selling locally-grown vegetables; two butchers were selling meat, some of it organic; there were cheesemongers, bakers, an olive-seller, and one stall that seemed to sell a bit of everything, from apples to vine-wrapped cheese. It was in the care of a well-wrapped person with vermillion hair curling up from under a woolly hat, a leather jacket over their protective layers, plaid trousers with chains hanging from the belt, and army boots. I stopped by the stall to buy some jam and a bar of soap, and glancing at the shelf behind the seller, I saw some bottles of clear purple liquid. The seller caught my glance, and said,

"I can't sell you any sloe gin, since I don't have a licence. Those are for collection."

"I don't think I have ever drunk sloe gin," I said. "Do you not need a licence to distil, too?"

"Sloe gin's a liqueur. Mine is a tincture, because I don't add sugar. You don't make the gin, you buy it, and soak the sloes in it."

"They're the fruit of the blackthorn, aren't they?" I asked. I recalled visits to a rural-dwelling uncle, picking damsons, eating blackberries, cracking hazelnuts in my teeth. I never collected sloes.

"They are, and the devil to collect, with all the thorns. Want to try a mouthful of the gin?"

I was tempted, but said no. My car did not approve.

"Maybe I could buy a bottle off you next time," I said, and was immediately handed a card that read *Rocker and*

"It was a good year for sloes," said either Rocker or Fox. "These bottles are three years old, smooth as a baby's backside, they're all spoken for but give me a call, I'll let you know what I have."

I smiled and moved on.

Twenty-one

THE CAFÉ WHERE we were to lunch, The Pot and Kettle, was housed in what had once been a private dwelling—a rectangle of dressed stone, two storeys, with sash windows and a yellow door—and retained some of its domestic ambiance.

The tables were set out to my right when I went in, and I realised that the café was bigger than it looked, stretching out behind into a small and currently rather muddy garden. To my left was a long glass-topped bay of shelves, displaying quiches, salads, brown bread topped with salmon or cheese, and an array of cakes, some with additional labels announcing organic or local ingredients.

Theo and Thornapple were already in the queue so I followed them, and brought my sandwich into the bay window overlooking a small brick courtyard. There was a single table, where we settled ourselves comfortably and started our meal.

"Tell us about Millar from when you knew him," I said. "We have assumed that the reason he was killed arose from something he was up to now. Something active, like the puppy-farm or one of his relationships. But that doesn't seem to be getting us anywhere."

Theo shrugged. "He told me he was a property developer. He was always a very assertive sort of person, and made everything sound like a great achievement. You know the sort. The sort who spends a couple of summers on a building site and calls themselves a builder, or does admin in a doctor's office and speaks of their 'medical background'."

Thornapple and I were both nodding.

"That was Tony," she went on. "He told a great story, and it took years before I realised that when he said he was an entrepreneur that the word he was looking for was really *chancer*."

"Did he have business troubles?" I asked. "Any rows, any enemies?"

Theo was shaking her head slowly. "Nothing I know of that would have lasted this long."

She frowned at her forkful of quiche. I bit into a very delicious cheese and salad sandwich. Thornapple was eating local-tomato soup.

"He handled stolen goods at least once," she said, and ate the quiche. "That was the breaking-point. I woke in the middle of the night and found people moving boxes out of the house. To be fair, I think he might have been telling the truth when he said it was one time only. He was a chancer, but he had a very fine judgement of what sort of risks he would take."

"If he was cautious about risk," Thornapple said, "— goodness, this is good soup—I assume then that Millar would have been cautious in his dealings with the sídhe."

"In fact, I don't know much about that. He had nothing to do with anything across the borderland while he and I were together. I had just started translation work then, and of course I signed the Official Secrets Agreement when I first took on inter-world commissions."

Minority languages, she had said in Whalen's, and me thinking she meant Frisian or something.

"It wasn't until he came to Ireland, I think," Theo continued, "that Tony found out about the borderlands. He came over here during the economic boom. I found this out through friends of friends, but I think he was flipping properties."

For a bewildered moment, I took her words literally. Was this some Other World trick? Thornapple saw my confusion, and explained. It boiled down to buying properties to sell on at a profit. A cheap property, usually in need of renovation, is purchased, and once renovated, is sold on. During the boom, the property market was brisk, and perhaps not as well-regulated as buyers might have liked, so renovations could sometimes be pretty hit-and-miss.

"He got in with a consortium of some sort," Theo was dredging her memory, "some Germans were involved, a couple of other English, the rest Irish. It wasn't big, but they did a good bit of work. It wasn't until after that that I heard he was crossing the borderlands more often."

"He turned up on my registers more than once," Thornapple said, "which suggests that he was doing it by the book. Requesting passes to go over. A licence for some small amount of imports of minor artifacts."

"Meaning that either he was legitimate—" I started, and Thornapple finished, "—or he was sufficiently legitimate to avoid attracting attention to anything illegal. On the other hand," they finished the last of their soup, "if as you say, Theo, he had a fine sense of how to keep his own skin intact, he probably would not have misbehaved on the sídhe side."

Theo was frowning, pouring milk into her coffee. "He was cautious up to a point, when I knew him, but some years after he had moved over here, I had to get in touch with him over a property we had owned together. I went through a lawyer, but Tony got in touch directly, and we met. It was fine, but he was a lot—sleeker. Prosperous. He was a lot cockier, too. I don't know whether that would have made him careless."

"But he wasn't killed by the sídhe," Thornapple said with confidence, "or from anywhere on that side. That we know."

"Do we?" I asked. The question had not occurred to me because… well, it wouldn't, would it? But maybe we had overlooked something obvious.

"We do," Theo and Thornapple spoke in unison, and Thornapple went on, "If one of the sídhe had come gunning for Millar, it would be obvious. If the marrow had been sucked from his bones, it might have been the sídhe."

That sounded definite.

"Who did he flip these properties with?" I asked. Some very vague little idea was picking away in the margins of my brain. "Why did he stop? The market slowed down?"

"It was getting a bit big for him," Theo said, "too many people involved, too many with more money and fewer scruples. And one of the fellas that had started it had left; didn't like the look of the market. They were right, too, the crash came about two years later."

"You remember any names? Anyone in particular who he didn't like?"

"No, I don't think… no, wait a bit—who was that lad you mentioned earlier? Malcolm someone-or-other?"

"Malachi Stone?" I suggested. Theo nodded vigorously.

"That was it. Malachi Stone. He was the same sort of 'businessman' as Tony, but a bigger sort of player."

"More money and fewer scruples," I said. I knew little about Stone except that he turned up in the newspapers every now and then, all flash suits and veneered teeth, usually being charged (and often getting away) with some business or commercial misbehaviour. I wondered if the dog-theft and puppy-farming charge would ever be made and would it ever stick. I rather doubted it. Theo was still speaking.

"…a few changes from when they first started. Of the original consortium, I think only Tony was left when Stone joined them, Tony and a man called… oh, goodness, let me think."

Our plates were whisked away by someone with half a dozen plates already along one arm, and a coffee pot in the other hand.

"I can't recall many of them," she continued. "One was called BeeBee Honeyman, which was pretty memorable, but she was killed in a train crash—not a crash, a train derailed near Khalilabad in India. Boban, what was his name? Farkas, he left Ireland and I think went into politics somewhere. Someone else left the consortium around the time Tony did, but started working on more specialist renovations. What was his name? He was Irish."

Thornapple asked if we wanted anything sweet, and went to the counter to see what was on offer.

"What kind of specialist renovation?" I asked.

"Historical," Theo replied. I thought of Patricia Hopkins cautiously describing Millar also working on restoration, *heritage, you might call it*, she had said. I recalled standing with Niamh Bracken and Ivo at the party at Cotter's Lodge, talking about heritage buildings and special contracts.

"It wouldn't have been—"

"Collier," Theo said, astonished. "Oh my goodness. It *was*. Ivo Collier."

Thornapple arrived back with warm scones and butter.

"Who was Ivo Collier?"

"Worked with Millar," I replied. "Millar and Ivo were working together in the consortium."

"I thought he was a lot younger than Tony," Theo sounded doubtful, and Thornapple, distributing the plates and cutlery, asserted that what good genes had started, healthy living and vanity built upon.

"Did they have any special contracts at the time?" they asked.

"What actually is a special contract?" I asked, dividing my scone. "Sorry for interrupting."

"It's a regular working contract," Thornapple told me, "but as I am sure you know, humans tend not to speak directly when they speak of the *aos sídhe*, the people of the sídhe. They say *our good neighbours*. The *good people*."

"The *Gentry Below*," I recalled my maternal grandfather, "*Themselves*."

"The *noble people*," Theo added, "*our other neighbours*."

"In the same way," Thornapple said, "the humans are circumspect when they speak of any dealings beyond the borderland. They say they are working *over beyond*, that they have *a bright crew* working with them."

"*Special contract* is in the same family, then—it means humans working on the sídhe side, trading with them, something like that?"

Thornapple was nodding. "In a nutshell."

"I wonder," I said, buttering some scone thoughtfully, "here we have Collier and Millar again. Working on properties, renovation, all that sort of thing. Already there were two instances of Millar and Collier in conflict because Millar was skimping on quality."

"You're wondering that's where Collier's motive lies?"

"Exactly. Even if the earlier properties were not these special contracts. Maybe this isn't the first time that Millar brought trouble to Collier."

"But he only found out on the night," Theo objected. I said nothing, following a line of thought to and fro between Millar and Collier. With part of my mind, I saw the logic of her objection, but maybe Collier, like Hopkins, had a party-trick or two up his sleeves. Something a bit more than just magic mirrors.

We walked together back to the car-park.

"What's your plan, Jessica?"

"I have a vague little idea," I answered Theo, "I'm going to call in on Lorcan Fitzgerald. It may be nothing, but I want to ask him a bit more about Cotter's Lodge."

"Do you think he'd mind a second guest?" she asked. I said no, though I did not add that I was not sure how Delia would react to her belovèd's ex-wife on the doorstep. Well, I guess we would find out.

As we approached our cars, my eye was caught by the dramatic appearance of the Shanbaltin ruin against the murky clouds. It looked like an early 1990s rock album cover.

"It's almost Hallowe'en," Thornapple said. "If you have the chance, you should come down here tomorrow night. That building, that ruin, is not what it seems. It's a cover for something—older, we'll say."

"What happens on Hallowe'en?"

"It's transformed," Theo said. "I've seen it, it is magnificent. Of course, you have to be careful to stay on *this* side, but you can see it."

"Oh, lovely." I added, unthinkingly, "Who organises that? The Council?"

They both looked at me, but neither spoke. I realised what was meant, and was mortified.

"Something—older, we'll say, than the Council, then."

Thornapple laughed. "No wonder you are our very own Miss Marple. See you soon."

Twenty-two

Cotter's Lodge, Sunday 30th October

LORCAN FITZGERALD reacted to unexpected callers with something close to belligerence that immediately melted into geniality; like a guard-dog revealing its inner Labrador. His welcome for Pupsqueak was enthusiastic. His inability to get names right led him astray with even so short a name as Theo, whom he referred to as Thelma for the duration of the visit.

Karolina was not in the house, being away re-stocking her cabinet of medicinal herbs, but Delia came in at the sound of new voices. I wondered if there would be awkwardness between the recent girlfriend and former wife, but there was none. Delia proclaimed herself delighted to meet Theo, who sympathised with her on Millar's death and on his unethical use of boosters. Lorcan ushered us into the sitting-room, where armchairs were arrayed near the bow window.

Pupsqueak found a patch of sunshine on the carpet, and settled down to snooze. Delia offered us tea, and when she went to get refreshments, I said to Lorcan,

"I hope you don't mind—I want to ask you a few questions about this house. When you bought it."

"What do you want to know?" Lorcan was surprised, but added, "Is this something to do with the murder?"

"It's why I'm asking, yes. It's a long shot, though. You said that when you were buying Cotter's Lodge, you offered a lower price after you got the surveyor's report."

"I did, and would have been justified in offering even less," Lorcan's tone was bullish again. "Karolina felt sorry for the seller, but you know women, soft-hearted. But it cost a small fortune to get it fixed up. The electrics—lethal! Lethal, they were. The house came on the market because the owner, a bit of a DIY fiend so I heard, got shot out to his reward hanging a picture! His drill hit a wire, and boof! Gone."

"What was the owner's name? The electrocuted man?"

Lorcan took nearly a full minute to recall it, excusing the delay on the grounds that it was the estate agent he recalled.

"MacArdle," he said at last, as Delia arrived in with a tray. Lorcan bounced out of his seat, seized a small table from under the window, and dragged it forward. As Delia set out cups and saucers, Lorcan added,

"J.J. MacArdle. Now, evidence in the house suggested that his DIY skills might not have been as good as he thought they were, so who was to blame, who knows. Accidental death, it was brought in as. We would have got a surveyor's report anyway, of course, but we made sure it was done good and proper. At the end of it, all I could think was it was a miracle the house hadn't fallen down already! Plumbing all arse-ways, electrics all over the place. Outdoor pipes shattered in that bitter winter we had, when was it? 2010? 2011?"

"Do you know," I asked, accepting a cup of tea, "when MacArdle bought the house?"

Lorcan crunched noisily on a gingersnap.

"I think," he said, halfway through, "let's see, we bought in… we're here, what, two years? Delia?"

"Two years this winter," she said, sinking into a seat. She was virtually unrecognisable from the *mimosa* her mother had so deplored.

"And he'd had it—I'm not certain, but MacArdle'd had it for ten years. Approximate figure only."

"You wouldn't happen to know," Theo said, and Lorcan leaned forward a little, smiling, "whom he had bought it from? Had it been renovated?"

Lorcan looked out of the window, thinking. It was Delia who answered.

"It had been," she said. "Remember, Da? The estate agent said there had been a few houses around in a poor state, but they were done up and put back on the market."

"You're right, lovely," said Lorcan, "that was it. Back when the country was throwing money around. Some crowd bought maybe four houses of this sort in or near Corrbofinn, biggish ones, going for the higher end of the market. They were all pretty tattered, from what I heard, so they were renovated—renovated! Some Slapdash Jimmy brought in, quality out the window so the work was done quickly, couple of coats of paint, and a smart new price-tag! MacArdle bought the house from the developers."

"What had the asking price been when you bought it?" I asked, almost impulsively, "I mean, did you have to reduce it by much?"

"A lot, yes. The asking price was somewhere around three or four hundred thou—you remember, Dee?"

"Asking price was four hundred and eighty thousand," Delia replied immediately. "You paid three hundred."

"Quite a drop," Theo was impressed.

"And this MacArdle man might have been electrocuted because of the shoddy wiring," I said, and Lorcan stopped chewing to say,

"I suppose he might. But I know they brought it in as accidental death."

"Do you know the name of the person you bought the house from?" Theo asked. "Did it go to anyone, anyone inherit? Or did the solicitor dispose of the estate?"

"Oh, it went to someone alright. I can't recall what relation, though. Nephew I think, or maybe niece. Not son or daughter. I can tell you who the solicitor was that handled the sale, but I don't know if he'll give you the name of the seller."

I doubted it. Whatever the solicitor might be obliged to tell the guards, a random civilian was a different thing.

We finished the tea, woke up Pupsqueak, and departed, or at least started the process of leaving. Lorcan kept drawing our attention to different parts of the ground floor of the house that had been fixed or improved. Theo said later that she wondered if he felt he needed to justify reducing the price, but I recalled Lorcan doing the same thing at the party. He was just very proud of his house, however gruffly he referred to things being done on Karolina's insistence.

While we were in the hallway, Delia suddenly said,

"This is probably a bit random but—I was just thinking. Say the murder was because of the house, the way the price dropped. Maybe they found out who was in the consortium."

"And came here to kill Millar?" her father said, a little derisively. His doting upon his daughter did not extend to removing the slightly mocking tone with which he responded to almost everything she said. "We knew all our guests at that party."

"The way you were handing out invitations?" Delia replied. Her doting upon her daddy did not extend to letting him get away with anything. "We had two werewolves here because you met them in a pub at lunchtime! You didn't know Jessica. And we didn't know this mysterious Bridget Earley person either."

"She might have been the person who inherited the house," I said, catching up with Delia. "She might have tracked down Millar."

"It sounds a bit melodramatic," Delia said, and Theo pointed out that the loss of almost two hundred thousand smackers could change a person's perspective on what was or was not melodramatic.

"Did she have the chance, though?" Lorcan asked, "The opportunity, as the detective books say?"

"I confess I did not really notice her," Delia said, and her father said, with a burst of belligerence, that we had Millar to thank for that.

"Normally, she's a crack-shot as a hostess," he told us, "just like her mother."

"I saw her… let me see, I saw her when she arrived," I said, "and then again standing over there, talking to Millar."

I pointed to the corner where the hallway to the downstairs lavatory and to Karolina's workshop met the main hallway where we now stood, leading to the front door.

"But I don't see how she could have administered it," I went on, "she wasn't handing out food or drink or anything."

"The guards don't know how he was given it, do they?" Lorcan said. "They even came around here to check how much atropine Karolina has. Went through her poison register, checked all her little bottles."

"They had to, Da," Delia said, "I mean, if there was the stuff in the house… but I'll tell you what was nuts," she went on, beckoning us down the hall to the cabinet of curiosities, "they were even into what we keep here in the cabinet."

She flicked a switch and a spotlight came on. Light twinkled along the edge of the silver vine I had admired before, across the gilt lip of the heavy-bottomed glass, and on the glazed face of a small porcelain human figure decorated with the outline of internal organs. Handy, I thought, you never know when you need to locate your spleen. The spotlights illuminating the contents of the cabinet very beautifully.

"We have this, you see," Delia pointed to the model of a belladonna plant with the shining berries, "and nothing would do the guards but to test it out and make sure that no-one could squeeze poison out of chunks of jet!"

Their little mandrake mannikin was still there in his felt suit. Lorcan saw me looking at it.

"They'd have had that lad lifted out and sent off to their laboratories if Niamh Bracken had met her end within spitting distance of us."

Theo and I left then, thanking them for their hospitality and for the information. We walked back to our cars, and as we unlocked them, I said,

"I wonder if that is a possible lead. There is no reason why Lorcan would know who had done the damage to Cotter's Lodge, but whoever inherited the house presumably would if they were a relative. They might have the names of the consortium involved."

"Why pick on Tony, though? Because he was handy?"

"That's a point," I said. "Of the names we have, only Millar and Collier are still here."

"On the other hand, it was Niamh, not Collier, who was killed."

"That's true," I sighed. It all seemed so hopelessly complicated. Still—faint heart never won fair murderer.

"Will you have time to complete your investigation, Mr. Holmes?" Theo smiled at me. "I heard you had ten days' leave."

"Oh!" I had forgotten I had told her neither of my newly unemployed state nor my decision to see out the remainder of the year in Herne's Acre. I gave her the update, and she looked surprisingly happy about it.

"I would hate to see you dragged off the scent," she said.

"I think I might just dig around a little more, see if the trail from a reduced-price house sale leads anywhere."

"Let us know how you get on," she said, opening her car, "I have to do a bit of work this evening, or I'd offer to help."

I waved at her as she drove off. Much though I wanted to turn Gwen's bumper for home and my trusty laptop, I was aware that my decision to stay in Corrbofinn until after Christmas meant that I needed to do some proper shopping. I had once—the first Christmas after Caleb died—been so disorganised that my gifts to my siblings all arrived late, and I dined off frozen fish and tinned soup on the day itself. That level of disorganisation would be outlawed in my new life. I would turn my attentions to Cotter's Lodge when I got back from Lissascaul.

I whooshed Pupsqueak into the car and drove off, wondering what a claret-eared dog would like to eat at Christmas.

Thornapple's Narrative. Licence Office, Sunday 30th October.

I was, as I always am, as good as my word. I was on duty that afternoon, and as soon as I got back to Licensing, I called Cray into my office. It arrived in looking sprightly, and my own cheerfulness dimmed. To be fair to Cray, and given recent improvements in its performance, I really should recommend it for promotion. But that would leave me with

Hixley, who was a toady, and who, if Cray was promoted instead of itself, would be a disgruntled toady. An impulse to selfishness had to be quelled.

I invited it to sit down, and I told it the latest theory as to who had killed Millar, but I had just started when Reception called—I have never become accustomed to their new system, where the receptionist suddenly materialises in the office—and said that Theo Solaita wanted to see me.

"You might already know this," she said, as soon as she was in the room, "but just in case you didn't. Jessica Quill lost her job. She lost her job, and she is going to stay in Herne's Acre until after Midwinter."

I was already rising up from behind the desk. I knew about the job, and I had hoped she would stay, but I could not quite believe it.

"You're certain?"

"She told me herself."

"We're in with a chance, then," I said, "we have until the Midwinter to convince her. If she agrees to become a Hosteller at Herne's Acre… Oh, this could be the answer to our problems!"

We each held out our arms with our wrists crossed, and holding hands thus, we began to swing, spinning until the office blurred and sparks flew. Breathless, we let go, and staggered happily apart. Only then did I notice that Cray was standing in the doorway with a tray of tea and buns.

"Chief?" it said, "I thought we'd celebrate."

Twenty-three

Jessica Quill's Narrative. Herne's Acre, Sunday 30th October.

THE DECISION TO STAY at Herne's Acre until the New Year brought a surprising level of relief to me. It was of course in part that I did not have to worry about finding a new job or an affordable home immediately. But more than merely relieved, I was almost *joyous*, in a way that I realised—with something like shock—I had not felt in a good two decades. It was not just that these unexpected extra demands had been removed. It was that for the first time in a very long time, I did not have any demands other than everyday life. Make sure your house is warm and clean. Have food, and cook it. Feed your dog, and walk it. And give it belly-rubs and reassurances that it is just *marvellous*.

Alright, everyday life at Herne's Acre currently included "find out who murdered two people before Butler decides it was you," but that was temporary. As soon as that little trouble was over, everyday life for the next few months at least would include sorting through all the contents of Hen Rosse's house, and exploring her garden. It still did not mean I could miraculously realise my dream of running a physic garden. But it did mean that, for at least a few months, I might not be in such desperate need of a dream.

When Theo drove off from Cotter's Lodge, I drove Gwen to Herne's Acre, and spent about an hour going through the kitchen and the utility room to write up a shopping list.

I had been living meal-to-meal and need-to-need because I thought that in a week or so I would be returning to my nasty little flat. Now that I had a few months here, I needed to set my home up properly.

The utility room contained more in the way of cleaning material and emergency standbys—extra light-bulbs, candles, batteries, fuses—than I had expected, and I only needed to add supplies for Pupsqueak, who needed a proper bed and water-bowl, as well as some toys and chews. The list of groceries for myself was longer.

Although I did not want to get carried away, and launch off on too enthusiastic a 'new life new me' jag, I felt it was as good a chance as any to put into practice something I had decided upon once the shock of leaving Louise had passed. Louise had liked to live in what she called a comfortable way, taking advantage of the easiest, most convenient ways of conducting her life: ready-meals, eating out, driving everywhere. Her hobbies were cinema and socialising.

I had enjoyed these sedentary pursuits too, up to a point (and not the socialising), but over the years she had put subtle pressure on me to only do things her way, engage with her hobbies. Looking back, I was irritated with myself for the passivity with which I had tagged along with Louise being Louise, without troubling to insist on Jessica being Jessica.

I trawled through my recollections and dredged up the ingredients for what once had been my most familiar recipes. I made a note to buy an Ordnance Survey map, and some walking boots. Socks, I wrote. Extra t-shirts. Even without needing office-clothes, I would later need to shop for add-itions to my ten-days-supply wardrobe, but that evil hour could be postponed. I wondered about my flat, and whether I needed to go back before Christmas to clear it out.

I wondered about Pupsqueak. He looked like a dog that would welcome exploring the countryside on paw. Which countryside was he accustomed to? If I followed him, would he lead me to Tír na nÓg?

I pulled myself together. The utility room had a collection of shopping bags, so I took a selection of these, checked my pockets for keys and the like, and set off for Lissascaul. Turning out of Pallasalee, I noted that I had not yet explored the village, I had not even been into the shop-and-post-office. I knew nothing of it other than Whalen's pub. Well, I would have time enough now to address that lapse.

The town was busy, and it took me a little while to get the shopping done, but I was finished by around six. I was tired, and it was a Herculean struggle not to buy a pizza for dinner. I compromised; better doing the right thing eighty percent of the time than quitting because I did not achieve one hundred percent. I bought some fresh fish, and vegetables, but oven chips.

Back at the house, I fed Pupsqueak and introduced him to his new bed and blanket. I put all the groceries away, put the chips in to bake, and cut up the broccoli. I opened up the browser on my laptop, took a deep breath, and typed *JJ MacArdle death* in the search box.

MacArdle family regrets to announce the sudden death of Joseph James (J.J.) at his home in Cotter's Lodge, Cotter's Hill, Corrbofinn. The death announcements were all very similar. Devoted family man. Pre-deceased by his parents... brother... Deeply regretted by his brothers Tom and John, and sisters Norah and Lily... nieces and nephews.... grandnieces and nephews, a string of names starting with

Toms, Andreas, Emmas and Áines, and ending with Jaydens, Kaitlins, and Mias.

He sounded like a decent sort of a skin, did J.J. MacArdle, a civil servant by profession but an explorer by inclination from the sound of it, with his "boundless enthusiasm" and his habits of travel and "trying anything once."

The official report of his death, at least the published version, was brief and to the point. MacArdle had an enthusiasm for DIY, and was reasonably capable. He had carried out a number of renovations on his house, and while he was not a careless workman, he had perhaps an unwarranted confidence in his abilities.

No-one could quite rule out the possibility that he had removed some of the interior plaster for some reason and, having revealed the amateurish electrical work that had been done, decided he could do no worse himself despite having no proper training. *Google was good enough for him*, his sister had been inconsolable, *Google and a couple of YouTube videos, he thought he could do anything.* The court had been stern about the lack of regulation of building work, but there was insufficient evidence to say that MacArdle's death had been anything but a tragic accident.

To whom did J.J. MacArdle leave Cotter's Lodge? I had no real way to find out. None of the people associated with the murder was called MacArdle, but of course the niece or nephew who had been the inheritor could have had any name. Once I had finished eating, I brought my laptop upstairs to the plan of my investigation. To stimulate my brain, I poured myself a glass of brandy and stood with it, staring down at my lists of names, the bristling fans of notes attached to each, and the speculative lines between possible causes and effects.

Niamh Bracken had been involved in property, in buying and selling. She had wanted Herne's Acre. She had been responsible for trying to get Herne's Acre a reputation for being haunted. But Herne's Acre was different. It had this 'bridle path' business going on, a source of income for Niamh. Thornapple had made it sound like a rare and valuable (if deathly dangerous) thing. It was hardly possible that Cotter's Lodge had the same kind of value, and that Niamh had gone too far with getting rid of the owner.

No, that didn't even make sense. Manufacturing hauntings was one thing, she could hardly re-wire a house as a booby-trap. No Niamhs were listed among the grieving relatives. Not Niamh, then, killing off her relative to get Cotter's Lodge.

There were no Ivos mentioned either, but could Ivo Collier have had something to do with it? Could he—or indeed Niamh—have been not a relative but a partner of whoever inherited the house? That made it much more complicated. Speculation simply opened up more and more options, it did not narrow anything down. Could I dig up any more threads? Where to start? Back to my trusty laptop.

If Google was good enough for MacArdle, it was good enough for me.

It took a long time. I matched every name on my investigation plan—Niamh, Millar, Jamie, Ivo, even Molly Thompson, Gemma Broderick, Patricia Hopkins—to Cotter's Lodge and searched the internet. That took long enough that Pupsqueak was whimpering to go out for a wee, so I went out into the beautiful clear night, and found my way across the night sky to Orion's Belt and the North Star while Pupsqueak watered the yard. I returned to the fray armed with a cup of tea and two biscuits. I went back down my list of names, and scoured social media for any sign of them.

And eventually I found a connection. Not one I was expecting.

It was past midnight, Pupsqueak was asleep at my feet. The house was cold, so I had found a rug to wrap around myself, and had a second brandy. I was pursuing Patricia Hopkins through the byways of her past timelines, and my goodness, did she have a lot of social media presence. An early adopter, was our Patricia, and an enthusiastic photographer, so my eyes were sore and gritty when I wound up on the Koré's World website. Almost idly, I started a new search.

And up she popped. Photographs taken on sunny days at Cotter's Lodge, of a man who was presumably J.J MacArdle and his grand-niece leaning against the bridge near the house, of them and another woman of MacArdle's vintage outside the little cottage that now belonged to Delia. #RIPUncleJJ.

But in that case, why had her name not been included in the list of mourners? I went back to Koré's World and went through the biographies again. I could not find the connection. I took a break, sat with sleeping Pupsqueak to watch an episode of *Murder, She Wrote*, and drink a cup of tea.

Just before the big reveal, I remembered that Koré's World, and Cotter's Lodge, and the people I was searching, had another link. I went back, not to my own computer, but to the records of Herne's Acre.

Hen Rosse had issued certificates to the attendees of her herbalist course, and she kept copies of these in box-files in her immaculate office. I settled down for a search, but in fact, it only took me about ten minutes to find them. Each certificate had been issued using full legal names: Patricia Marian Hopkins. Gemma Angel Broderick. And Andrea Regan O'Moore.

Regan had been the seller of Cotter's Lodge, the Andrea who had "sadly missed" J.J. Disappointed to the tune of one hundred and eighty big ones thanks to the damage wrought upon her inheritance by profiteering developers, one of whom had been Tony Millar, now deceased. The philosophical question was, would it be going too far to accuse someone of committing murder as a punishment? The practical one was: did she have opportunity to kill him? Had she been at the party?

I was yawning like a gorilla by this stage, and struggling to stay awake. At least, that was my excuse for why the obvious solution did not occur to me straightaway. I decided I would leave it until the morning, and face into it afresh. I woke Pupsqueak up and ushered him to his basket, then I washed my teeth and crept off to bed.

It was three o'clock in the morning when an answer—possibly *the* answer—came to me. I still did not quite know *how*, but I was fairly confident I knew *why*, and I was very close to finding out *who*. I could only have been asleep ten minutes when I woke up, woke completely up, as refreshed as a daisy with a dose of dew on it.

Why could Regan not have been at the party? Why could *she* not have been Bridget Earley? Bridget Earley in velvet boots with clear heels decorated with gold foliage. And in what unsuitable footwear had Regan crossed my yard when she came to view my house? All together now: violet velvet books with clear heels and gold foliage. I was utterly convinced that I was right, and I fell back asleep undisturbed until almost half-eight the next morning.

Happily, it was only then that I began to worry about how on earth I could prove it.

Twenty-four

Monday 31st October.

IF I HAD REMAINED in the morning as convinced of the accuracy of my guess as I had been in the wee small hours, I would probably have gone without delay to Birhanu to tell him what I knew. But after a sound sleep, and in the cold light of day, I began to have doubts.

Regan had seemed perfectly ordinary when I met her, and murder—especially one done in cold blood and for no benefit other than the satisfaction of a vengeful impulse—seemed so terribly extreme, so operatic a suggestion. I got up early, thinking over the problem. I picked away at the idea as I made breakfast, and tidied the kitchen afterwards. My determination to improve my eating habits did not, I knew, mean I would be sticking to some regimented dietician's dream. For that reason, I had included in my shopping the ingredients for what had been a favourite of mine when I lived alone: boiled fruit cake. I thought while I baked.

Thornapple appeared at the door in the middle of the morning. At first, they said they would not come in—"we're on my rounds, just called to see if there was any news"— but asked me if I would join them for lunch in Whalen's.

"I know it's twice in two days, but there is something we need to ask you."

We were at the kick-end of October, today was Hallowe'en and had a muddy sort of light not uncommon at this time of year. It had rained during the night, and the clouds had a sort of tremulousness about them that suggested that they might yet visit further showers upon us.

All the same, I decided to walk rather than drive to the village, less because I thought I might have a drink and more because part of my Herne's Acre Resolutions was to get back to walking. A mile and a bit in one of the flattest parts of Ireland was not exactly conquering Helvellyn, but it was more than I usually did, and that was the point.

Thornapple helped me off with my coat, told Pupsqueak he was marvellous, and introduced me to their companion.

"Cray, meet Jessica Quill. Jessica, this is Cray—it is indispensable to me in the Office."

Cray, it has to be said, does not in any way echo Thornapple's effortless, haunting beauty. Its skin is a sort of muddy green, and its features look distinctly squashed. But it has marvellous eyes, unusually large, and bright and clear like brown glass, and a peculiarly cheerful smile. As soon as we had sat down, Whalen came over with the menus. Thornapple had just told me that Theo would join us shortly when the door opened and Theo arrived along with a brisk north wind. Once she had settled in, I blurted out,

"I think I know who it was pretending to be Bridget Earley. And who killed Tony Millar."

They listened with flattering attention while I explained how I had arrived at Regan O'Moore, but there we returned to the old problem: when did anyone have the opportunity to slip Millar the fatal dose?

"Where did you see Tony before he died?" Theo asked me.

"Even without thinking of who, where did you see him?"

I pushed my empty plate away, and stared at the floor, trying to dredge up the times I had seen Millar, and in the correct order. Cray, I saw in the corner of my eye, scribbled them down as I spoke.

"In the hallway, being hissed at by Trisha Hopkins, who threatened to cut his throat. In the sitting-room, when Jamie nearly choked him with a slab of fruitcake, which if it had worked might have been the most unexpected weapon in the history of murder. In the hallway when he was speaking to Ivo. Then he passed me in the conservatory when he went outside."

"Millar? Or Ivo?" Cray's pen was poised.

"Millar. That was about the time that Ivo must have been outside looking at the cottage. The next time I saw Millar was inside the house again. Jamie told me Dermot was looking for me. Millar was in the hallway, at the corner where the hall to the front door meets the hall to the downstairs lavatory. He was talking to Bridget Earley, or Regan O'Moore as I now think it was. Dermot and I started saying our good-byes, and by the time I went outside, Millar was nearing his last breath."

Cray said something, but I didn't hear. I was picturing Millar chatting to Bridget Earley, in banshee outfit and her purple velvet boots, smiling and flirting. When could she have given him poison? In what? Was there some *woo* involved? Some advantage she had because of the 'true nature' of Corrbofinn?

In that fickle way of the preoccupied mind, I recalled in brief flashes the conversation where Thornapple, Theo, and Whalen told me about Corrbofinn. Shaking hands with Thornapple. Whalen putting away the shot-glasses he had lent to Lorcan. Pouring pints, saying *on the house.*

Saying, *You might as well be drinking petrol.* I had never much liked shots. *Might as well be drinking petrol as tequila.* Or atropine?

"No," I blurted out, startling my guests, "Whalen had never been away from the bar long enough for anyone to poison a drink—no, he had been! He was away reuniting Ivo with his dropped wallet. It might not have been long, but it might have been long enough."

Millar and Bridget—Regan—had been standing on the corner of the hallway, right beside the little sunroom that was being used as a bar. Bridget had been swinging a shot glass between her fingers.

"How about this?" I asked rhetorically. "Regan, got up in her Bridget disguise, is standing in the hallway, flirting with Millar. I saw her, and I saw her with a shot-glass in her hand. How about this: the atropine into a shot-glass, with just enough tequila to mislead an already drunk person? And an interaction with an incorrigible flirt, enough to persuade him to take the glass and toss the drink down his throat without noticing?"

There was a silence while they absorbed the idea. Then I added,

"But that's Millar's murder. I don't know why she would have killed Niamh. Unless Regan also wanted to buy Herne's Acre, but that's a bit weak. Damn."

"Remember what Niamh said before she died?" Theo said eagerly. "Not the thing about the fetch, but the other words. You thought she was just delirious."

"Well, mandrake has that effect. She was talking about hills."

"Hills," Theo said, "and bridges. But how about Bridget?"

"Bridget Hills?" Thornapple said, but I caught on.

"Heels!" I said, and Theo nodded at me.

"She saw Regan at your house, tried to put her off buying it, telling her about ghosts. Remember she commented on her boots? Talked about how she had worn velvet at the party, and it was raining? And that odd quip about Regan making an *early* bid?"

Twenty-five

IT SEEMED SO SIMPLE a connection that I kicked myself for not having spotted it. Niamh was, or rather had been, fashionable. She knew what a Blahnik was, she could spot a Caveletti at a hundred paces. Niamh had not been delirious, had not been rambling about landscape features. She had been speaking of Bridget Earley, and of Regan O'Moore, and of how she connected them via the distinctive heels of their footwear.

"Though how to prove it?" Thornapple said. "Everything will have been cleared up after the party. There's only your word about what kind of shoes this person was wearing."

"The only thing I can think of," I said, "is that Regan O'Moore must have planted the wig and glasses in my workshop. Maybe there're fingerprints there."

"Maybe," Thornapple sounded hopeful, but Cray said,

"Though the worst that would mean was that she had been in disguise and tried to blame you."

"It's a start though," I said, firmly. "I'll add these new ideas to my detective plan when I get home."

The gangly youth came and took away our plates.

"There is another reason I asked you to join us here," Thornapple said, folding their hands on the table and turning to me with a rather formal air. To my alarm, Theo also shifted in her seat, as though in preparation for something: an interview, or a ritual. Cray opened a new page in its notebook, and smoothed it. Even more alarming, the pub became very quiet.

Thornapple flicked a rather reptilian and very bright orange tongue over the thin froth on their upper lip, and smiled at me.

"I understand congratulations are in order," they said, and when I looked blank, they added, "Your redundancy."

I was about to protest, but I recalled my feeling of relief. At the same time, I did not know how much Uncle Tim's annuity would yield, and I did not expect miracles.

"Congratulations might be going a little far. I still have to find a new job. Unless you have a private income for me in your back pocket?"

"Let us see," they said, reaching around their own back, and bringing out a tiny purse, like a clamshell made of soft floral cloth, fastened with a clasp of two blunt-tipped spokes clipped over each other. They flicked open the clasp, and reached in, pulling out all sorts of odds and ends: a small lamp, its shade fringed with amber beads, a bandana, a telephone made of black Bakelite, the receiver attached by a plaited cord, a ceramic platter with a mosaic of a fish painted on it, a small cylinder made of coloured glass. Then they peered into the purse, and shook their head at me.

"No private income, I fear," they said, turning the purse upside down, then rapidly packing all the items back in again. "But I could give you a better offer."

I was too astounded to speak.

"I am encouraged," Thornapple went on, "by your describing the workroom as *your* workroom. We have heard on the grapevine that you have decided to stay in Herne's Acre until after Midwinter. You no longer have a job. You no longer have a partner. You no longer have a home, only a roof over your head."

"Well, thanks for that summary of my life." I could not avoid sounding a little despondent.

"Your life is not over, so it is not a summary. It is one way of looking at where you are on the road. You did not like your job. Your siblings may have been more clear-sighted than you about the person you lived with."

"You told me about Caleb," Theo said, "and your uncle Tim told me when your father died. That was two big losses in five years."

"You may not have been making your best decisions," Thornapple said, and I had to admit, though not aloud, that they might have had a point.

"We don't raise this subject in order to assess your past self," Thornapple went on, "but to see if you have an interest in making new decisions. Making a new life for yourself, as it were. We might all be able to help each other."

"How could you need my help? You can travel through the ether and cross boundaries into other worlds!"

"It's on almost exactly that point that we need it," Thornapple said. "Let me explain."

What Thornapple was offering me was, of all things, a job.

There was a collection of framed photographs on the wall behind Thornapple, and the glass reflected the customers behind me, all of them half-turned in our direction, pretending not to listen.

"What would that be?" I asked. Thornapple leaned over, and the table rocked on uneven legs. I performed the familiar duty of folding up a beer-mat and shoving it under the short leg.

"When you phoned your office, or Beelzebub's Coalface,

as I believe you called it, you found that you never have to see it again. That they have to pay you a little more redundancy than anyone thought. That's how much we wanted you to stay."

"And you finally remembered the terms of Timothy Fennimore's will," Theo said. "You had forgotten about the annuity."

I felt a full-body thrill, as if gently electrocuted. I did not know what to expect.

"Furthermore," Thornapple said, "I can offer you a job."

I looked at them.

"Now don't build up her hopes," Whalen said from behind the bar, "the pay is lousy."

The other customers laughed. I turned around in my seat.

"But is it enough?"

"That's the attitude," said one of the men at the bar, striking one hand against the other. "More than enough is a waste."

"You would have certain—privileges," Thornapple said, "that would reduce the demands on your purse. Your employer, for example, would pay certain of your bills."

"You still won't have much to make whoopee on," said another customer. I laughed whole-heartedly, and said,

"I commute three hours every day to spend seven hours in a job I hate, in the ugliest office I have ever had the misfortune to see, with people who are either disillusioned, devious, or dolts. How much whoopee do you think I make as it is?"

I turned back. The feeling of recklessness that had unzipped my usually self-effacing tongue in the face of the guards' unfair accusations came back.

"What's the job?"

"Herne's Acre is a crossing-point," Thornapple said, sitting back, "between this world and the world of the sídhe. You saw part of what that crossing-point looked like when you were dreamwalking."

"How do you know—"

"Because we are all dreamwalkers, those of us who tend the border between the worlds. All of us can step into different times and places. All of us are able to walk into those multiple realities that others only visit, and recall only in fragments. You have been a dreamwalker since you were a child. So was your mother. So was her brother Tim."

"Uncle Tim worked for you," I said, realising it as I spoke. Thornapple nodded.

"He did, and he is a terrible loss to us. But he was a diplomat. What we want you to be for us is a Hosteller."

"A hustler? Me? I couldn't hustle an after-dinner mint."

"A *Hosteller*. Herne's Acre is a Hostel, a place of rest for travellers. You would have help, of course. You would just need to look after Herne's Acre on *this* side, and coordinate with the *other*, and everything will sort of… sort itself out."

I had never had so vague and unlikely a job offer in my life. The exact duties, the nature of my employer, the nature of my contract, even the pay—nothing was pinned down, nothing spelled out, nothing definite. Who used the Hostel, what help would I have, what Thornapple meant by *the true nature of Herne's Acre*, remained up in the air. Bizarre.

Thornapple laughed.

"I will leave you to think about it, JQ," they said, "but we have to go now. Cray and I will be on high alert in the office from this afternoon."

"Why?" I asked, standing when they stood, and Cray said,

"Samhain. It's Hallowe'en tonight. We'd better get going."

I don't know if I had just become more observant or if they were taking less care now that I knew the "true nature" of Corrbofinn, but Thornapple and Cray had both definitely faded from sight before they even reached the door of Whalen's pub. Looking out of the window as we pulled on our coats, Theo said,

"There's a lot of rain in those clouds. Do you want a lift home?"

"I won't take you out of your way," I said. "Even if I get caught in a shower, I'll dry off back at the house."

"It's not out of my way, I'll just go to the B&B from the other direction."

Theo delivered me to the front gate of Herne's Acre ahead of the rain. As she pulled away, I ran across the yard to the workroom.

I had found the wig and the glasses in the press, and I stood with my hands on my hips, looking around for a likely surface to have captured any kind of a finger or handprint.

Immediately, my eye fell on the stainless-steel counters that ran the length of the wall, just below the presses. When the wig had fallen out and hit me in the face, it had fallen to the floor, and with part of my mind I had noticed that it had some cobwebs clinging to it. Between two of the counters was a gap, and I wondered if that would be a place to start my search.

If the wig had fallen there, then a natural way to keep your balance while you reached for it would be to put your hand on the counter. There might not be anything, of course, and Cray was right that even a fingerprint would demonstrate only that Regan had been in the workshop, which she openly was when she came to view the house. It would help only if we could demonstrate a connection between 'Bridget Earley' and the crimes.

There definitely did seem to be some kind of a mark or smear on the surface. I took out my phone quickly, but before I dialled a number, I hesitated. If it had not been so important, I would have almost certainly said it was a hand-print, but I was not at all sure it was enough to show to the sympathetic Birhanu, let alone Butler.

I started to put my phone back into my pocket, but as I did, I recalled Theo saying that she had seen the cover before. It was not so astonishing that she had, since it had been commercially available. On the other hand, Trisha Hopkins had bemoaned the fact that they had not sold well. I looked at it again. It was, I thought, too ordinary. Too much familiar Goth cliché.

Yet Theo might have been right, because now that I was dredging my memory for everything that might relate to either of the murders, I had a feeling that I, too, had seen it. Or maybe just many things *like* it—but no, it was a definite sense of familiarity. Everyone at the party had had a phone, but I didn't think it was from there.

I closed the door of the workshop behind me, and dashed across the rain-battered yard to the house. When I was shaking the rain out of my coat, my phone rang. It was Theo.

"I've remembered where I saw the phone-cover. I was at your house when both Niamh and Regan were there."

"I've just remembered too," I said, "I saw it, too. The same one, I think. At Shanbaltin in September, when I got lost. The woman I asked directions from, she had her phone in that cover."

Twenty-six

Thornapple's Narrative. Commission Headquarters, Monday 31st October.

HALLOWE'EN IS PHENOMENALLY busy in the Commission as a whole and in Licensing in particular. We're run off our hooves—or whatever, we pride ourselves on being diverse—and it didn't help this year that Sigune was half distracted with trying to find homes for the three remaining pups that had not made the cut for the sky-pack. Once she gets her fangs into something, Sigune is like a hound on a scent herself. Nothing short of the offer of food will distract her attention.

That's my excuse, at least. It's not that I didn't listen to Cray, but I had no capacity to really pay attention. *Leave it with me*, I had said, when it came to me with what was puzzling it, *I'll check it out*. And I meant to. But I thought it had just got the wrong end of the stick.

Even Cray admitted that it was not sure about the implications of what it had seen. Theo on her way to Shanbaltin. Well, nothing wrong with that, though it was a rather risky time to visit, what with Hallowe'en. The Veil is very thin, faded to a thin nothing once the sun dips just so far below the horizon, diaphanous tatters is all that is left, and the sídhe really let down their hair: it is their night to party, their night to roam the world, and the humans had better keep from their path or the devil would take the hindmost.

But Cray had come to me when there was still time before twilight, when the balance of the world would shift, let alone before nightfall.

I had to keep Cray's snout to the grindstone, too. I could see its squashed little face get more and more anxious, but we were supposed to be getting Ambassadors out of the line of fire, not investigating murders. That would keep till tomorrow. Or so I thought. I had underestimated Regan O'Moore's capacity to strike while the iron was hot.

Jessica Quill's Narrative. Lissascaul and Herne's Acre, Monday 31st October.

I had almost forgotten that it was Hallowe'en until Thornapple mentioned it. I had no idea how people in Corrbofinn would mark the occasion. I wondered if they would do the kind of trick-or-treating that had been occasional around Kirkaller, though I had a feeling that was more a United States tradition, whereas I remembered my late father recalling his youth—children and adults going round to houses but in order to perform in some way: singing, or telling a story, dancing, or, in my father's case, playing a tune. That was, I now recalled with an almost sentimental shock, how he had met my mother. I thought I should have some refreshments to hand, should anything of that nature happen tonight, so I drove to Lissascaul to stock up.

I was astonished at the supermarket. It was decorated for the season, but I had never seen anything like it before. I had become accustomed to garish masks, to masks based on figures from cinema, to carved pumpkins and skeleton outfits, spray-cans of cobwebs. Childish things, things that were symbols of 'the spooky season', nothing more. Walking into a Corrbofinn shop at Halloween was a very different story.

The masks on display were properly apotropaic, like the masks that Birhanu's search team had worn into the poison garden, the masks that he said were "effective against many things." I had never seen sheelagh-na-gigs for sale, and I cannot deny that I was a little startled to glance up and see a row of them available in reconstituted stone.

They were less eerie than the serried ranks of pre-carved turnips, some already illuminated from the inside with candles, to show off to full effect the blunt, rectangular eyes and the stretched approximation of mouth and teeth. There were no skeletons, though a couple of shelves labelled *Rocker and Fox Handcrafts* included animal skulls—cat, badger, rabbit, and fox (each one conscientiously labelled as roadkill, with the date of their demise). There were plenty of candles, plain wax and coloured, with some sigil or other stamped into the wax.

I really was not sure with what, if anything, I ought to decorate Herne's Acre given what Thornapple had explained about its proximity to the borderlands. I played it safe, and though I bought some candles, I mainly stocked up on food. There were apples with marzipan filling that could be baked, I bought peanuts, walnuts, and a coconut; there was brack, there was a sort of kit to make "no-fuss toffee apples." And I bought some cocoa and dark chocolate. I had no way of knowing whether I was buying too much or too little.

As I reached the last aisle, I passed shelves full of disposable partyware, paper cups and plates, and I recalled Lorcan Fitzgerald's party, and the fact that he had borrowed glasses from Whalen's pub. It seemed a much more sensible approach than serving wine in paper cups, or shots in plastic containers that looked better suited to mouthwash than tequila.

I wondered, with a little fizz of excitement, if I was right that the atropine had been given to Millar in a shot glass. By the time he had died and the guards had arrived, all the glassware that was not in use had already been washed—Whalen was extremely efficient. There was no way to check a glass for fingerprints or traces of atropine...

Or was there?

I stopped dead in the middle of the aisle, staring vacantly at a shelf of mannikins made out of willow, and some lethal-looking "threshold guards" made of blackthorn.

I was speculating that Bridget Earley had killed Millar, and that she had done so with a poisoned shot of tequila. I had seen her speaking to him, leaning against the wall, swinging a shot-glass between her fingers. If she had just poisoned him, then I had seen her holding the murder weapon, in a manner of speaking.

Very slowly two and two were coming together, and they might even make four. Would Bridget—Regan—have put the glass back in the kitchen? What if she had not, in case someone noticed? In case the body was discovered quickly and the guards came to forbid any further cleaning?

I could recall the shot-glasses with their glinting rims tumbling upwards from Whalen's hands onto their shelves. And I could recall seeing just such a gilded glass where it had no business being.

I added a bottle of spiced rum to my groceries, paid for the lot, and went home, still picking away at my idea.

I had put away my purchases, and just decided that I would risk making a fool of myself by ringing Birhanu about my idea, when I was startled as the radio came suddenly to life.

This is a public service announcement. The future victim is currently at Shanbaltin, on the site of the former church there. Theo Solaita, originally from Byker in Newcastle upon Tyne, now resident in East Lintzfield, believes she can assist a murder investigation by determining whether or not belladonna grows in the burial ground in Shanbaltin. Her investigative partner, JQ, believes that the woman who gave JQ directions when her sat-nav cut out due to the properties of Corrbofinn was none other than Regan O'Moore, a.k.a. Bridget Earley. Someone is following Theo Solaita to Shanbaltin, and there is a chance that they mean her no good.

I did not stop long enough to wonder if I recognised the voice. I had my phone out of my pocket in a moment, and I rang Birhanu. I told him about the print, or at least partial print, that I had found on the steel counter in the workroom, and what it was that I thought it meant. He listened without interruption, and when I had finished, he said,

"Even if it is a print, and even if we can match it, it won't prove anything about administering poison to Millar, or feeding mandrake to Niamh Bracken in a glass of wine."

"Not by itself it won't," I agreed, "but if you don't mind taking a chance, I have an idea. I think Regan left the murder weapon in Lorcan's house."

"Hit me," he said, and I was relieved that he sounded curious, not resigned. I explained my idea, and he listened without comment. When I finished, I said,

"There's one other thing."

I have no love for stories where the action arises from a character doing something very stupid. The people in a horror film who hear a terrifying noise and part company to investigate. The amateur detective who does not tell the police that they, too, are following up a lead.

Ten days ago, I would not have been so calm about telling another person that I had heard a very weird news report on a self-activating radio. But Birhanu lived here, so I did not hesitate. I told him about the announcement I had heard (it sounded to me like Cray's voice, but I did not say so in case it got into trouble for hijacking the airwaves), saying that Theo was in danger in Shanbaltin. Birhanu said immediately that he would get some crew over there and follow on himself from Cotter's Lodge.

Where I did, perhaps, make a bad call was to grab Gwen's keys. Birhanu sounded like he was on the move as I was speaking, I was sure he would get his crew as he called them to Shanbaltin immediately. But if Theo was being in some way threatened, it was most likely by Regan, though how Regan knew where Theo was going was not a question I could answer.

If Regan was our murderer, then she was clearly dangerous. On the other hand, the people she had murdered had been poisoned. She had not been dangerously violent, she was not armed, she did not shoot people, or throw knives. It seemed to me that once we did not accept any cocktails, glasses of wine, or shiny apples, neither Theo nor I would be in particular physical danger. I did not think I was going to save the day or anything, though I expected to get there faster than the squad cars, simply because I was closer. I just did not want Theo to be alone in a confrontation with a murderer.

I grabbed my coat, and rushed out of the house. Pupsqueak was in the back seat before I could stop him, and would not get out again. I cursed my lack of foresight for not having any way of contacting Thornapple or Cray. Maybe Birhanu did, though. That thought cheered me up, and I switched on Gwen's radio just in case anyone from the *other side* had anything else to tell me.

Twenty-seven

Shanbaltin, Monday 31st October

THE ROAD FROM Herne's Acre to Shanbaltin usually took about twenty minutes to drive. But what I had forgotten was the bridle-path, and the differences wrought upon a borderland by Hallowe'en.

I drove Gwen over the bridge and turned east. It was later in the evening than I had realised, but as I became more accustomed to the roads, I had become less timorous. There was still plenty of light by which to see what were becoming familiar surroundings: the outline of the trees marking Herne's Acre boundaries, the sweep of the road up to a large farmhouse with a fine squash-patch in front; around the corner would be a smaller, very old house with an old stone barn and a small yellow tractor.

But no sooner had we passed the corner where Herne's Acre met Heathcote, whence I had seen Niamh Bracken fleeing and her goblin-raiders scattering at the approach of Themselves, than the landscape changed. The dark through which we were driving now was suddenly denser, and nothing to left or right of me was familiar anymore. There were more trees, for one thing, bigger, sturdier trees that were not thick with ivy. The sky was not clotted with clouds, and the canopy of stars was very bright.

I could glimpse what looked like lights from windows in amongst the trees, and here and there I saw the silhouette of an animal—cattle mostly, but there were a few horses too, and at one point I had to slow Gwen right down to let a heavily-antlered stag cross the road. When I set off again, I remembered that in winter, it is the female deer that have the antlers. Sorry, Dasher. Now and then I saw a pale swooping smudge among the dark branches, and guessed they were owls. It wasn't until I noticed that the road itself was wider and had fewer potholes that I suspected we must have crossed the borderlands into the world of the sídhe.

I turned right after the Garrytost Crossroads, and drove slowly through Shanbaltin village, my eye already drawn to the orange moon and the rise of the hill, watching the weird phosphorescence outlining the shape of the ruin.

Thornapple and Theo had not been kidding about Shanbaltin being transformed. The light had all but faded and the trees around the building and along the horizon were blunt blocks of shadow. It was approaching sunset but the moon was already rising; a full moon, which struck me so forcibly that I slowed the car down on the empty road to look at it. Hallowe'en full moons were very rare; not only that, but I could have sworn we had already had a full moon. A blue moon, and a full one, all on Hallowe'en? What were the chances? Or whose moon was I seeing? It was low in the sky and very orange, like Thornapple's eyes, but the road was a sand-pale slash between the dark bulk of the hedges.

I set off again, rounding a corner down the hill towards the ruined ch… towards the brightly-lit construction of shifting walls and blazing towers, glowing windows gouged into black shadows, the sky and the stars seeming to flicker above it. I felt weak as water and tempted to bolt, and had it not been for Pupsqueak, straining forward from the back seat, every sense alert, I might very well have turned tail there and then.

I slowed down further so that I could find somewhere to shelter my car. Just as I pulled into a recessed gateway, my phone beeped, and I saw I had a message from Theo. My heart leaped with relief—she was okay! I could break for the border without being a coward!—but even as I opened it, I realised that I did not believe it. *Meet me at Shanbaltin. There's something odd here.* I bet there is, I thought, and I fear I am about to find out what it is. If Theo had sent me that message, then I was an elf.

I set off for the building, or whatever it was, giving Pup-squeak firm instructions to stay where he was. The weird light made the dog's bone-white pelt shine, and his emerald eyes sparkled. His very ears glowed like rubies. He whined at me, quivering, but stood still by the car. I should have brought him to an animal rescue before now, I chided myself, instead of postponing it just for the company, and now running the poor animal head and neck into trouble.

I made my way towards the gateway to the building, where I had parked all those weeks ago to ask for directions. The burial ground looked much the same at first glance— honestly, I am not sure if I was expecting open graves— but the peculiarity that I gradually noticed transpired to be that the ground level was much lower than before.

The air looked fragmented, or, rather, it looked crystal-ised, so the fractured and refracted lights and the shifting shapes made me dizzy. I wondered which idea was worse: going through the gate, or climbing over the wall? Each seemed dangerous. Hedging my bets, I walked along the outside of the wall, wondering if I could find an accidental opening that might not be perceived as trespass.

There was a section of the wall that was slightly crumbled, and that with a bit of effort I could squeeze through. The wall, about two feet thick, was much higher than I recalled, and I felt a spasm of claustrophobia at the thought of pressing myself through the narrow space. But squinting through it I saw something that made my decision for me. Theo's car was parked in amongst the blackthorn trees, now bigger than I recalled and jagged with thorns.

The shifting, dizzying light was sufficient for me to see Theo slumped in the front seat. Here we go, I thought, squeezing my eyes shut and myself through the narrow opening in the wall, so much for thinking Regan would stick to poison as a weapon. She may already have killed Theo. Was this is the hill I die on? Insofar as I had time to wonder, I wondered what Regan's intention was. To kill Theo and frame me? Or to kill both of us? Such thoughts, on an ordinary day, would have seemed absurd and rococo but here, with the inexplicable moon and the shifting reality of Shanbaltin, it all seemed chillingly likely.

Nothing ate me before I reached the car, at least, so that was good. I opened the door, with all sorts of booby-trap scenarios cluttering my thoughts. Theo was breathing normally, but she was unconscious—the consequence of the dreadful swollen cut on her head—so I did not dare to move her. A sudden flare of light from Shanbaltin caught my eye, and the silhouettes of tall and angular things moved through the fracturing air. A surge of something I did not recognise but that I expect was raw terror made me lean back into the car and shout at Theo, in the faint hope she would react. She did not, so I reversed out, shutting her door as quietly as I could. But not quietly enough.

The moment the *clunk* of the car door sounded, two heads popped up over the roof of the car. Right, I thought, I had better get a wriggle on. The two heads, which were at least attached to separate bodies, had peculiarly bright eyes, narrowed in an unfriendly way. I turned, but before I could run, two more figures, different ones this time, moved gracefully towards me. Gracefully, and very, very swiftly, like bright red rugby wingers.

I bolted, and out of the shadows came Regan O'Moore, sensibly shod this time, leaping like a lion in shoes that meant she could take down a fully-grown and not at all gazelle-like Jessica. As I hit the ground and the air left my body, I tried to recall what Olive, practising for her brown belt, had taught me. I went limp in Regan's fierce embrace, which she was not expecting. I kicked my legs out and hooked her ankles with mine, so when I pushed up and over, she lost some of her balance.

Regan was strong, but she had not been expecting retaliation. She let go to re-grip, but it was long enough for me to get one arm free. I swung my elbow back, cracking her across the bridge of her nose with a satisfying crunch. The language out of her was appalling. I was shocked, I can tell you.

I am not quick or light on my feet, not these days, but I was back on them as fast as I could, turning for the road. The brief spat had brought us to the attention of others… or rather of Others, and I had a bad feeling about how They would welcome two humans brawling on Their night. Before I had run twenty yards, I felt a crushing pain in my back, and I staggered, falling heavily. I barely managed to roll over. I could not imagine what I had done but it felt like my spine had been twisted out of place.

Regan was striding towards me, holding out her arm, with some blocky item gripped in her fist. It had a blue aura shimmering around it, and by that dim light I saw it was wood, polished, carved, and bound at points with metal coils. A wand? She covered the ground between us in seconds, and knelt beside me. I was certain she would kill me. Better make it worth it.

I took my deepest breath, braced myself for the pain, and lunged, grabbing her eyes and face in my clawed hands. At least Butler and Birhanu could get skin samples from my fingernails. My attack did not make Regan drop her wand, but it did break her concentration, and the severity of my pain dropped. I scrambled to my feet. A sudden and bright light behind me startled me. I turned, and looked up.

I wondered if *making eye-contact with the sídhe* was an unremarkable cause of death in Corrbofinn.

Twenty-eight

Thornapple's Narrative. Licence Office, 31st October.
THERE IS PLENTY of warning about the differences between the spinning of the human world and the world of the sídhe.

The most famous is time. Countless travellers to the sídhe, or fairyland, or whatever it might be called, think that only a short time has passed but, when they return to the mortal isles, they have been gone for centuries. I think that Regan O'Moore had counted on this to dispose of Theo. Theo knows the language of angels, she is a hard woman to kill, and Regan would most likely have come out the worse of a direct encounter.

But Theo had voluntarily gone to Shanbaltin, right onto the border between our worlds. If, poised between them, she was rendered unconscious just long enough for midnight to pass on the sídhe side but not on the human side, she would be trapped in the gap where the worlds are thin enough to see one into the other. I don't know what would have happened, not exactly. I have heard it would be like falling into a black hole in the universe. The humans, I believe, describe the effect of that as *spaghettification*.

Really, I think it is the end of the road for Cray in Licensing. We were absolutely flat out, haven't seen anything like it in years, and we had not a moment to spare for the humans. We thought, in any case, that everything was in hand. Cray has been in Licensing so long that it really knows its way around all our systems, it's familiar with all sorts of quirks of our legislation, it has become very confident in managing—what shall I call them?—the stronger personalities encountered by our office.

Cray was in demand from all quarters, all afternoon. I had been asked to take on a couple of interns; they had just spent three weeks in my boss's administrative office, so they had as yet to be introduced to hard work. They were nearly in tears by mid-afternoon until Cray stepped in and took pity on them. It packed them off for a tea-break while it covered the Issue Desk whence we handed out the Border-land Passes that had already been approved.

One of the arrivals was Patricia Hopkins, with a favour to ask: she was hoping to take up an unused pass, issued for Regan O'Moore, who was no longer able to travel. We don't encourage this kind of chopping and changing, mainly because the paperwork is a pain.

But Cray had its wits about it. Under the cover of making small talk while it was busily stamping forms and signing the backs of authorisations, it asked,

"So why can Regan O'Moore not use her pass?"

"She murmured something about *bright business*," Patricia said, then added cheerfully, "It sounded very highfalutin', but if you ask me, she just wanted to bunk off and see the light-show at Shanbaltin."

As soon as Patricia left, Cray dashed to the Watcher's Tower. Theo, not being a reckless sort of person, had told us she was going to Shanbaltin and Cray could see her creeping about through the shrubbery in front of the Great Hall. It flipped the scryers to a wider view, and saw that Regan O'Moore had used the crossing at Herne's Acre onto the bridle path. With commendable presence of mind, Cray had seized the radio microphone.

On my second encounter with the Gentry Below—or, the Gentry Right In My Line Of Sight as they were rapidly becoming known—it was Theo, not Pupsqueak, who saved me from being shrivelled. She had regained consciousness as soon as Regan was separated from her wand, it having been magic, rather than concussion, that had kept her knocked out. The moment I looked up, and despite a lump the size of Skellig Michael on her head, Theo rugby-tackled me to the ground, thus saving my skin from becoming my lining.

Squinting under one of Theo's arms, I could see that Thornapple, Cray, and an enormous figure I found out later to be Sigune, were already in mid-diplomatic flow. I had glimpsed an agitated line of figures, large and angular, as I hit the ground. Sigune's voice was distant, rumbling and mellifluous, and evidently also persuasive. Thornapple came hurrying over while Sigune, arms stretched wide, was urging the Others back towards the main door of the Great Hall. There was some resistance, but Sigune seemed to be in her element, and carried all before her.

"You can let her up now, Theo," Thornapple said, and Theo let go. We both sat up.

"Where's Regan?" I asked, spitting mud and bits of gravel out of my mouth.

"She's headed back along the bridle-path," Thornapple said. They sounded exhausted, and their skin was a noticeably paler shade of blue. "There is nothing to worry about. The last thing I did before leaving the office this evening was to sign emergency passes for Birhanu and Butler. She won't get past them."

I got up, very shakily. My mouth was swollen and throbbing.

"Let's get you home," Thornapple said, and looked around. Gwen's lights came on, and the engine started. The car rolled gently over to me, and the driver's door opened. I was enchanted.

"Is this because I drove her across the bridle-path?"

"I think," Theo said almost apologetically, "it is the result of a hound from the Wild Hunt Sky Pack sitting in her back seat for a week."

"Pupsqueak!" I exclaimed. "A Wild Hunt Sky-Pack pup!"

He wagged his white tail and looked modest. We climbed into the car, and Gwen drove me home.

I don't know how the others managed, but they were at Herne's Acre before me. Usually, I would not have been so accepting of six guests (and only three of them human) making themselves at home in my house in my absence. But I was so delighted to find the fire warming the kitchen, and dinner warming in the oven, that it seemed the only reasonable way the evening could have gone. Besides, if what I dimly understood Thornapple to have explained about Herne's Acre was correct, it was not exactly private property.

Sigune was considerably smaller than she had been at the Great Hall in Shanbaltin. She seemed to flicker a little, like a hologram glitching. Sigune's face—or at least, the one she was wearing—was hawklike down to the yellow eyes, the Samuel Beckett eyebrows, and the third eyelid. She was built along Sidney Greenstreet lines, and in the green-and-bronze velvet clothes she wore, she looked a bit like a ship's figurehead, but with lichen. It was she who had brought the bottles of Veuve Clicquot champagne. I limped in, battered, muddy and sore, and Sigune boomed at me,

"A glass of the Widow for the returning hero!"

It was now about ten at night, time having jumped on the human side for those of us returning from the sídhe, and I had had no food since lunch. I really could have eaten a horse between two bread-vans. Thornapple was producing plates of food to order—I asked for the first comfort-food I thought of, mushroom bourguignon and mashed potatoes —and Cray handed them around.

I curled up on the settee with Pupsqueak on my feet and my dinner-plate on my lap. Theo and Sigune kept the glasses topped up, while Birhanu attended to the fire, and Butler eyed me beadily, flipped open her notebook, and said,

"We had better get through the drawing-room scene before we all get langered."

A sudden vision of Butler getting tipsy while watching a Golden Age detective gathering all the suspects together in the drawing-room made her seem a little more human and a little less scary. Cray brought a plant-stand to the side of the settee, and put a glass of champagne on it for me.

"Thornapple said you came across the border after Regan O'Moore bolted," I said. "Did you get her?"

"Of course," Butler sounded almost offended, and I was glad that Thornapple distracted her with a plate of curry. "We were starting on the same track," she added, helping herself to chutney, "but we were a bit thrown off by the Niamh Bracken murder. Regan O'Moore was at an event in Kilduff the night that Niamh was killed, we could not work out a way for her to get to Pallasalee and back again when her car was within sight of CCTV all night."

"I only thought of the explanation when I was on my way to Shanbaltin," I said. "Patricia Hopkins told me about the Koré's World event that evening. But there is a train from Kilduff to Cotter's Hill."

"But no bus," Birhanu said from where he was adding wood to the fire, "no taxis."

"Regan had been at Herne's Acre offering to buy it," I said. "What if she told Niamh she wanted in on the whole risk-tourism venture? That she'd buy and they go into business together? Might Niamh have agreed to fetch her from the station, maybe they'd both go across to the bridle-path?"

Butler did not look convinced, but Birhanu, dusting off his trousers, took out his notebook and wrote something down.

"Then," I went on, "after she killed Niamh, Regan made her own way back to the station."

"How?" Butler said. "Niamh's car was still there."

"How about Niamh's bicycle?" I finished my champagne. "The night I met the Others on the bridge, Niamh and her clients scattered out of my field. Niamh cycled away. But I didn't see any sign of her bicycle when I was there the night she died." A memory suddenly came to the surface. "And I passed a cyclist on the road as I was driving to Niamh's."

"Regan took it, you mean," Butler said, "cycled back to Cotter's Hill train station, and dumped it somewhere."

I nodded.

"My guess, but it's only a guess, is that she dumped it near the train-track," I said. Birhanu screwed up his eyes, thinking.

"Near the train station, if you are agile enough, you can go over the bridge and down to the track," he said, looking at Butler. "If O'Moore dumped the bicycle there and hid it in the long grass, who would think of looking?"

Butler whipped out her phone and told some underling to get down to the station and start the hunt.

"Why did Regan kill Niamh?" Birhanu asked, over the sound of his boss's irate voice demanding *What do you mean what colour? How many are you expecting to find?*

"That's no way to tell a story," Sigune said. "Remember I've only been treated to the crumbs of it from Thornapple. Too busy keeping my... nose... to the grindstone, haven't you Thornapple? Charming Jessica, do a weary diplomat a favour. Start at the beginning. For me."

Sigune leaned over with the Widow by the neck, and replenished my glass.

Twenty-nine

"It started I suppose some years ago," I said, trying not to bolt my mushroom bourguignon or mashed potatoes. "Regan O'Moore inherited a house when her great-uncle J.J. MacArdle died in a domestic accident. Move forward a couple of years, Regan puts the house on the market. Lorcan Fitzgerald gets a surveyor to look at the house. Surveyor heard about MacArdle's death, and apparently was curious as to how MacArdle had managed to hit a live wire, given where he had been drilling. So, the surveyor is very thorough, and unearths all sorts of problems that had managed to stay hidden since the house had been renovated and sold to MacArdle."

I stopped to eat some more. Thornapple picked up the tale. "Lorcan Fitzgerald still wants the house, because his wife loves it, but the price is too steep because he will have to renovate. He offers a lower price, and O'Moore has to accept it. She is now quite certain that the renovation work that Millar and his consortium had carried out was responsible for her great-uncle's death. She is also very angry at the reduction in value of her inheritance."

"And to be honest, she is a bit of a sociopath, no?" Theo said. "To actually *murder* someone out of revenge. For no reason other than revenge. She gained nothing from killing Tony except knowledge that she had punished him."

"Well, they do say it is a dish best served cold," Sigune remarked, applying the champagne bottle to every glass in reach.

"It was certainly cold. I don't know when she got onto Millar's track, or whether she was planning to off anyone else from the development consortium that was flipping properties."

"We won't know until her lawyer arrives," Butler said. "She's in custody but saying nothing. My guess is that Millar was the only one of the consortium who was still borderline criminal, still ripping people off."

"Collier is legit," Birhanu added, "He left the consortium earlier than Millar, he might have been gone before they did the work on Cotter's Lodge. O'Moore started her revenge long before now, she had to track down who sold Cotter's Lodge, and who did the damage to it."

"Did Regan know Tony?" Theo asked. "How did she find out where he was?"

"She lives in Kilkenny," Birhanu told her, "but she is from Corrbofinn, and she commutes here for Koré's World work."

"Lorcan didn't mention knowing her personally," Butler added. "The house sale went through an estate agent, and solicitors. Her name would have been on the deeds, but he had no reason to remember it. It would have been easy enough to hear about Millar, since he was still living in Corrbofinn, and she heard that he had started a relationship with Delia Fitzgerald."

"Then she met Gemma Broderick," I said, "I presume accidentally, in the shop that Gemma works in."

"Gemma was a direct link to Millar," Thornapple added, and Cray piped up,

"Also a fall-guy, since she'd have a motive when she found out that Millar was dating someone else."

"Enter Bridget Earley," Theo said. "Am I right?"

I nodded.

"I expect it was her best chance at getting within reach of Millar," I said, "but once she abandoned the disguise, there'd be no evidence of a connection between Regan O'Moore and Tony Millar. She found out about Millar's personality from Gemma."

"Did she get the belladonna from the poison-garden here?" Cray asked me, and I shook my head. I had thought she probably did, as she had been at Herne's Acre often enough to know what poisons were around. But Theo had worked it out. It had nearly got her killed.

"She found belladonna growing wild at Shanbaltin," Theo said. "It was sheer chance I thought of it. They have a farmer's market in Lissascaul on Saturdays, and when I was there, I was talking to Rocker."

It took me a second to remember: Rocker and Fox Farm Produce, where I had bought jam and soap.

"I was chatting to Rocker, she had some customers picking up their bottles of sloe gin," Theo was saying. "She was giving samples, too, and when I took one, she mentioned it was a good year for sloes. Someone else in the queue was a forager, and said something about people not picking the sloes in Shanbaltin. Rocker sort of laughed, and said no-one ever dared pick the sloes there."

She paused, looking at me. The silence went on, but then I remembered.

"When I stopped for directions!" I exclaimed. "It was at Shanbaltin, at the ruin. The Great Hall. The person I asked directions from said she was picking sloes."

"I knew I had seen that Koré's World phone-cover before," Theo went on, "and you said it was familiar to you, too."

"I thought at first that it was just that the image was very generic, but of course, yes, I recognise it now."

"But I had seen Regan O'Moore with one. That time I dropped in here," she turned to Butler and Birhanu, "when Regan and Niamh were calling, I saw Regan with it then. I wondered what it might mean if it had been Regan Jessica had seen in Shanbaltin. So, I thought I would make a trip out there, to see if belladonna grew there as well as sloes. I let Cray know what I was doing."

"How did Regan know where you were going?" I asked. It had not occurred to me before.

"You'll never guess who was in the queue ahead of me," Theo replied, "picking up a bottle of sloe gin."

The chanciness of the encounter startled me, but I saw from the others' faces I wasn't alone. Sigune whispered something to Cray, who got out another bottle of champagne.

"This Regan O'Moore made her atropine dose from the belladonna," Sigune prompted me. "And…?"

"Then someone—maybe Patricia, but someone—told Regan about Delia's party. Regan took the chance. She invited Gemma, knowing Gemma would almost certainly see Millar with Delia. Her idea, I think, was to be at the party at the same time, in her Bridget Earley get-up. If Gemma had a decent bust-up with Millar, then Regan would slip him the poison, and leave Gemma holding the can."

"Why was she late to the party?"

"We're not sure," Birhanu answered Cray, "but when Jessica told me her idea, I checked the traffic reports for that day. Just on the off-chance. A lorry broke down on the road from Kilkenny and caused a three hour delay. That might have been it."

"But Regan was so late that Gemma had gone," I continued. "She went ahead with the murder anyway. She didn't use the ampoule, though."

"What did she use?" Thornapple pounced.

"She used," Birhanu said, "the one bit of concrete evidence we have."

He held up a large plastic bag, and in it was the heavy-bottomed, gilt-rimmed shot glass that I had seen in the Fitzgeralds' cabinet of curiosities. I had seen Bridget Earley with Millar only once. She had been leaning against the wall at the corner of the hallway to Karolina Fitzgerald's work-room, and Millar had been leaning just that little bit too close to her, smiling and flirting. He was drunk. The party had started in the afternoon and once the drink began to flow, Millar was soused.

Whalen had been away from the 'bar' only momentarily, but it had been long enough for Regan to dodge in, doctor a shot of tequila with a shot of atropine, and have it to hand. She struck up a conversation with Millar, who would have flirted with a pig in lipstick, and flirtily gave him the shot, laced with belladonna.

"Luck wasn't with her, though," I said. "She probably expected to be away from the party quickly—no-one knew her, after all, she could slip out easily. But Whalen came back before she could return the glass. I don't know why she did not just leave the glass somewhere for Jamie or one of Whalen's helpers to pick up and wash—"

"She might not have wanted to take the chance," Birhanu said. "If she had changed her plan from using an ampoule to dosing a drink, and her scapegoat Gemma was gone, she had not planned how to dispose of a glass."

"Now that we can narrow down the time," Butler said, "the statements are being checked again, to see if anyone recalls speaking to a banshee around the time in question. She might have been planning to leave immediately, and was delayed. You know what parties are like."

"Then," Thornapple added, "Millar did not take very long to die, and Birhanu was at the party. The guards arrived probably sooner than Regan expected. She couldn't clean the evidence off the glass, she couldn't take it with her in case she was searched."

"So she hid it somewhere among other objects on display," Cray said, "the cabinet of curiosities at the end of the passage."

"And there it stayed," Birhanu said, "beautifully covered in fingerprints, until Jessica said I should take a look in the cabinet. We also have a handprint from the steel counter in Hen Rosse's—sorry, Jessica's—workroom. It does not exactly prove that she put the wig and glasses there to reinforce the idea that Jessica was Bridget, but that is the least of our worries."

Butler's phone buzzed and flashed. She asked a few terse questions, and ended the call.

"You were right about the bicycle too," she said to me, "they just found it. At least, they found *a* metallic-red sports bicycle dumped on the side of the tracks. I suspect it will be Niamh's."

Thornapple asked, "Did Niamh know something about Murder's millar? I mean Millar's murder?"

"The visit to Herne's Acre wasn't too lucky for Regan," I said. "Theo recognised her phone-cover, Niamh recognised her shoes. Niamh was interested in fashion, in designers. She did not recall seeing Bridget Earley, but she said herself that she remembered the boots, if not who was in them. When she gate-crashed Regan's so-called buyer's visit, she recognised the boots immediately, and knew that Regan was Bridget. She didn't necessarily guess that Regan had anything to do with the murder, but she might have. Clearly, Regan was not taking any chances."

"She didn't go with atropine again, though?" Sigune sipped her champagne.

"She probably could have, but I think she had already decided that, as I was an outsider and Gemma was no longer useful as a scapegoat, I would be the one she would frame."

"That's why she used mandrake," Birhanu said. "So the weapon came from Herne's Acre."

"Regan contacted Niamh," I speculated, "maybe saying they could work together with the bridle-path, something like that."

Birhanu's phone buzzed. He listened, said *yes* several times, and ended the call.

"Ma'am?" he turned to Butler as he got up. "O'Moore's lawyer has arrived at the station."

Once Birhanu and Butler had left there was silence, and a slump in energy. Thornapple had begun to look less pale, but I began to be aware of my own exhaustion. Theo yawned, and Cray rested its chin on its arms folded on the table. Only Sigune seemed undimmed by the passing of time.

"Tell me, Thornapple," she said, "have you managed to get the Staffing Office off your back? Made your recommendation for promotion?"

Thornapple looked unaccountably delighted.

"Given Cray's performance in the course of the last few weeks," they said, "naturally, I offered it the option to have its name put forward for promotion."

"Promoting Unfortunate Cray leaves you with Insufferable Hixley. Explain your current expression of delight."

"Cray is disinclined to move away from the Licence Office," Thornapple said, and Cray added,

"Hate to see the place fall to chaos without me."

Pupsqueak trotted around the kitchen, which I was beginning to learn indicated that he needed to go outside. I started to get up, but Theo waved me back to my seat, and let Pupsqueak out the back door. I emptied my champagne glass, and put it on the plant-stand.

Pupsqueak started to bark in the distance. I wondered dozily about the cause, but there were plenty of night-animals around Herne's Acre that could have caught his attention. After a few moments, the tone of the bark changed, and became higher, faster. I had not heard that before, and I began to unfurl myself to go and see what was the trouble. I had barely set my foot to the ground when Pupsqueak let out a string of yelps.

I was on my feet and across the kitchen in a moment. Everyone rushed to get out, but Sigune was ahead of us all. By the time I reached the door Sigune was steaming across the yard at a rate of knots. Thornapple shouted her name, but with the air of knowing it was a lost cause. They hesitated, but a glance at Theo and Cray seemed to confirm a decision. Thornapple began to usher us all back inside.

"Quick," they said. "Quick, now."

"But—"

"He crossed the sídhe," Thornapple said, "not for the first time. Sigune's true form is not for the unprepared."

Cray shut the door behind us, and Theo locked it. After a moment of absolute silence, there was a short crack, an explosion that sounded electrical. Then a sound, loud and strange, a blare of trumpet with a rolling, roaring growl. Silence. And past the window, Bernie Reynolds and gangling

Paudge pelting like mad things up the road. There was no
sign of Malachi Stone, nor was there ever again.

Thirty

I CAN'T USUALLY sleep during the day. But after so hectic a
Hallowe'en, and having been up half the night, I managed it.
I fell asleep sitting on the settee with a mug of tea in my
hand. I woke up at four in the afternoon, curled up under a
rug, with Pupsqueak asleep beside me. I had slept for a
solid twelve hours.

Pupsqueak woke up with me, and bounded down, stretching and yawning exuberantly. He had his waking wits about
him a lot quicker than I did. I bumbled about groggily,
stumbling to the kettle to make tea. On the island I found a
small casserole dish that I did not recognise. Stuck to its lid
was a note in handwriting I did not recognise either. It read
*We hear you solved the murder! Congratulations. We hope
you enjoy shepherd's pie. Heathcote.*

There was another note, too, this one from Thornapple.
I brought it with me as I strolled outside with my tea-mug
in my hands and Pupsqueak at my heels.

It was already turning to twilight again. The day evidently
had been overcast and damp, and the clouds had acquired a
sort of dirty bronze sheen that suggested heavy rain incom-
ing. The air was fresh, though, and I inhaled as deeply as I
could. *Apples somewhere*, I thought, *blackberries long past
their best, the herbs in their sheltered garden, the sweet smell
of belladonna in my poison garden.*

I looked at Thornapple's note. *We'll be in Whalen's tonight.
Join us.*

I recalled the vague and unlikely job offer Thornapple had extended. The lack of detail about the job of 'Hosteller', the identity of my employer, the duties, salary. The uncertainty about *the true nature of Herne's Acre*. I thought about the job I had just lost, the dingy flat, and the noisy, untidy house I had shared with Louise. I thought of Louise, and her highly-strung slipper-dog. I thought of Caleb, the museums, and of the Bethune physic garden I had so admired. I thought of the unbroken quiet of the mornings at Herne's Acre, and the peace I had forgotten I found in solitude.

Pupsqueak set off sniffing busily around the yard. From where I stood, I could see the inky crowns of Heathcote Woods, and hear the raucous colony of rooks calling to each other as they circled together, and descended back into the trees. A few scouts, like soot-flakes on the discoloured sky, set off to round the stragglers back to the rookery. Across the field to the poison garden, the twilight was curdling to darkness. A fox trotted out of the shadows in the field. I just had time to identify its silhouette and admire its fine brush, before it disappeared into the trees. I turned back to the house.

The light from the kitchen dribbled into the yard, and so Pupsqueak was standing right in the brightest spot of the whole yard to wee. This was *a* true nature of Herne's Acre, of Corrbofinn, I thought, whatever else Thornapple might have to tell me.

I read the note again. *We'll be in Whalen's tonight. Join us.*

More Books by R.S. Maxwell
(writing as Susan Maxwell)

'Hibernia Altera' Sequence
And the Wildness (Flux Avellana #1)
Good Red Herring (Muinbeo Chronicles #1)
A Wild Goose Hunt (Muinbeo Chronicles #2)

Other
Hollowmen
Fluctuation in Disorder

And the Wildness
(Flux Avellana #1)

"So the actual reason I was calling you is because—get this —I am not going to Prague this summer at all. Surprise! Thanks, Villa. Just ruin my life for me."

Villa Grace is in disgrace. Her expulsion from school has ruined the prospect of a family holiday in imperial Prague, where her mother is organising a conference. Two of her three siblings are barely speaking to her, as all four face into a 'holiday' sweltering on Cobwell Farm in the back of beyond of drought-stricken Hibernia.

But the power-hungry St. Maur Ker family has breached the border between mortal and sídhe for their own gain. Cobwell, on the threshold of myth, is about to become the centre of a battle between older, wilder forces and the technomantic ambitions of one of the empire's great aristo–corporate clans.

Caught up in this conflict, the children are forced to face up to the dark underbelly of their parents' corporate environment, and to confront their own conflicting ambitions and loyalties.

For readers of all ages.

Good Red Herring
(Muinbeo Chronicles #1)

"Some of these stories really started decades, generations, ago, and now come to their close. New things begin to arise from the past, like phoenix feathers separating from the flame. The winding down of the old stories and the starting of the new arose from a death; a murder, if you will believe such wickedness. We warn you. We are the last—eh—people to pretend that Muinbeo is some kind of Island of the Blessed."

Those enigmatic entities, the Storytellers of Muinbeo, know that History has something waiting in the wings. To set the scene for their audience, they relate a gripping tale about a death and its consequences.

When her mentor is bitten by a rogue werewolf and "joins our hairy brethren howling at the moon", apprentice detective Salmon Farsade is assigned to Hal McCabe, Detective Chief Inspector and vampire, just in time for a murder.

Fen Maguire has been stabbed, throwing the normally peaceful community of Ballinpooka into shock. The investigation into her death lifts the lid on more than just the name of her killer: political corruption, Outland conspiracy, academic deceit, and plain old-fashioned greed. A second murder follows: the clock is ticking, and as they seek a key to unlock the truth, the detectives are both helped and hindered by the various human and not-so-human beings that populate Muinbeo.

For readers of all ages.

Irish Times Best books of 2014 for children and young adults

A Wild Goose Hunt
(Muinbeo Chronicles #2)

"You did not tell the Abbess a single lie," Diamond said, "But you didn't tell her the truth."

As a good Sombrist, Hunter Sessaire is aware that not only lying, but curiosity, is very much frowned upon by his community. As an apprentice archivist, he cannot resist the temptation to puzzle out how a manuscript could have been stolen from a room within the Sombrists' Labyrinth. A room that opens only during a planetary alignment. An alignment that has not yet taken place.

But this is not the only enigma abroad in Muinbeo. Seemingly disparate occurrences remain opaque even to those normally in the know. Detective Chief Inspector Hal McCabe is scratching his head over the inexplicable vanishing of his apprentice, Salmon Farsade, and the dramatic and destructive theft of an ancient silver hand from the local school museum.

The boundaries of Muinbeo, carefully managed to keep the Outland and its machinations outside, where they belong, have become a bit more porous than McCabe would like. Not least when he begins to suspect that some of the uncanny events may have their roots in a controversial Outland archaeological dig in Aegypt… Once again we are led into a maze of mystery by those not entirely reliable narrators, the Storytellers, in this enthralling sequel to *Good Red Herring*.

For readers of all ages.

Hollowmen

"It seems to me—and I no longer claim objective recall—that the morning on which I first arrived in Quettopolis looked much like this morning just breaking. One year ago. I was right at least that it was my last job."

The Moufet Institute's mission is to protect endangered lepidoptera, but its experts are becoming bystanders, sidelined by the 'Players' and their pursuit of corporate self-perpetuation. Cuffe, recruited to create the rhetoric to underpin a new corporate vision, finds her initial confidence eroded by the peculiarities of the Institute and its environment—the punitive *process* with its absent defendant, the disregarded but omnipotent Registry, the quarterly Hunt, the Forest as it re-asserts itself.

Then the Institute is galvanised by the discovery of a breeding pair of a rare moth species in a country in the throes of a military coup. The Institute in turn is riven by competing ambitions—the scientific specialists trying to save the moths, the Players trying to save the goose that lays the golden eggs. Meanwhile, no-one has been paying enough attention to what is happening in the basement…

Hollowmen is an intricate and unsettling work, its shifting, interleaved narratives in turn ironic, lyrical, witty, and savage.

Fluctuation in Disorder

An encounter with an alien enemy. A strange epiphany in a
fog-bound park. A collector of the names of the dead faces
their own death. Rebel divinities respond to the prayers of
despairing creation for deliverance. Bureaucrats find their grip
on reality dissolving in odd ways.

In these ten finely crafted and unsettling stories, Maxwell's
slipstream style interweaves strands of naturalism, science
fantasy, and the experimental irreal, illuminated by sharp
flashes of wit and language of lyrical precision. Many of
the characters exist in a state of slippage, alienated from a
world they thought they knew by an encounter with something that is indifferent to them, but to which they cannot
remain indifferent.

More than twenty years separate the earliest and the most
recent of the stories in this collection, but certain persistent
preoccupations provide loose thematic links—environmental
crime and retribution; the ways, both overt and insidious, in
which institutions can corrupt or sacrifice those within
them; the interpretations and recording of past events by
unreliable narrators; and the pervasive, irreducible weirdness
of existence.

If you enjoyed this book…
…please consider reviewing it online.

If you want to follow me online…

Website: www.biblioref.com
Blog: bibref.blogspot.com

LibraryThing: librarything.com/author/maxwellsusan-1
Goodreads: goodreads.com/dr_susan_maxwell

Mastodon: @BiblioRefuses@mastodon.ie
Bluesky: @bibliorefuses.bsky.social
YouTube: youtube.com/@biblioref

Linktree: linktr.ee/dr.susan.maxwell

www.ingramcontent.com/pod-product-compliance
Lightning Source LLC
Chambersburg PA
CBHW010341170726
48283CB00009B/2913